A cool, fun, fun...
Cathy Cassidy

It's complicated . . . Kitty's life, that is. I was rooting for her all the way!
Karen McCombie

A lovely book. I really like the fact that in a low-key kind of way, without huge drama or major issues being signposted or thrust down people's throats, it just gently gets on with being what it is: a straightforward and very sweet story about first love. We need more books like this out there.
Liz Kessler

A lovely story that's realistic, moving and full of warmth — I really enjoyed it! Luisa Plaja

It was a delight to read and felt like a being wrapped in a blanket of cuddles. Wonderfully honest and, as always, Keris Stainton is just perfection as a writer. Sister Spooky

Perfect mood-busting book which I read with a huge smile on my face right the way through. YA Yeah Yeah

I could easily sit here all day and talk about how amazing STARRING KITTY is, but to be honest, you should just go read it for yourselves! Readaraptor

Bravo to Keris and Catnip for this wonderful little book which is heartfelt and gorgeous throughout. I cannot wait for the rest of the series. The Overflowing Library

Look out for the next story about
Kitty, Sunny and Hannah:

SPOTLIGHT ON SUNNY

Out Spring 2015.

KERIS STAINTON

STARRING KITTY

For Harry

CATNIP BOOKS
Published by Catnip Publishing Ltd
Quality Court
off Chancery Lane
London WC2A 1HR

First published 2014
1 3 5 7 9 10 8 6 4 2

Cover design by Tim Rose

A CIP catalogue record for this book is available from the British
Library

ISBN 978-1-84647-184-1

Printed in Poland

www.catnippublishing.co.uk

1

Kitty saw Dylan as soon as they walked into the café. She was at the side on one of the high stools by the little window shelf. Even though she was sitting in, she had a takeaway cup and Kitty desperately wanted to know what was in it. Probably coffee. She imagined Dylan drank coffee, not hot chocolate. Probably proper coffee too, not the puny one-shot lattes Kitty drank sometimes. Dylan was wearing black leggings and the shiny purple Doc Martens Kitty had seen her in before. And a denim jacket. Her hair was a sort of purpley-red too, with a silver scarf tied around it.

'Er, HELLO!' Hannah's face appeared right in front of Kitty's. 'Are you not listening? I asked if you wanted a drink. Sunny's in the queue.'

'Sorry,' Kitty said, shaking her head and feeling her cheeks hot up. 'Sorry, I was thinking about Mum.'

The lie came so easily that it made Kitty blush even more, particularly when Hannah did her head-on-one-side sad face. 'Hot choc? I'm paying.'

'Er, no, sorry,' Kitty said, trying not to look at Dylan. 'A latte, please. Just one shot.'

'No probs,' Hannah said. Then she leaned her head closer to Kitty's and said, 'I thought you were staring at Sam.' She grinned.

Kitty hadn't even noticed Sam was in the café. She scanned the room and spotted him, slumped on the leather sofa in the corner by himself and looking at his phone. He glanced up and, yes, he did seem to be looking in their direction, but with his fringe hanging over his eyes she couldn't tell for sure.

'Oh yeah,' Kitty said. 'No.'

'He was staring at you,' Hannah said. 'Like this.' She flopped her tongue out of her mouth and panted.

'He was not,' Kitty said, smiling. 'And stop looking; he'll think we're talking about him.'

'We are talking about him,' Hannah said. 'And he totally was. You're not interested?'

Kitty wrinkled her nose. Sam was okay. Compared to most of the boys in Year 9, he was great – she almost never saw him trying to look down her shirt or up her skirt – and she'd once bumped into him coming out of the library and he'd blushed, which was cute. But was she interested? She shook her head.

'You could do a lot worse,' Hannah said. 'He's hot and he doesn't honk of Lynx.'

Kitty smiled. 'Yeah, I know. I just don't . . .' She shrugged.

'Well, you know. Keep him in mind. Do you want anything to eat? I'm going to get a muffin.'

'No, thanks,' Kitty said. 'Just the latte. Ta.'

Hannah headed over to join Sunny at the counter and Kitty returned to trying not to look at Dylan. She just couldn't seem to manage it. She told herself to look out of the window or down at the tiled floor, but her eyes kept drifting back to Dylan. The hem of Dylan's jacket was a bit frayed – it was probably actual vintage, not one of those new ones made to look distressed . . .

God, what if she was looking at Dylan the way Hannah had said Sam was looking at her? Her tongue wasn't hanging out, obviously, but what if everyone could see her thoughts on her face?

Since she couldn't seem to make herself do the easiest thing – not look at Dylan at all – Kitty decided the best way to deal with it was to look at her in sections, so that if anyone did notice her staring, she could say she was admiring her shoes or her hair or something. Just not . . . her.

As Kitty was wondering how Dylan got her hair that colour – could you dye it purple and then red? Or would you have to mix them and do them both at the same time? – Dylan turned and looked right at her.

Kitty immediately felt her face burning and she wanted to kick herself. Blushing was so embarrassing – why did her own face have to show her up?

Dylan smiled and hopped down from the stool. She pulled up the hood of her hoodie and threw a brown leather satchel across her body, before pulling her hood back down again and heading for the door.

'Hi,' she said as she passed between Kitty and the long table in the centre of the room.

Kitty felt so dizzy she actually reached out and grabbed the back of one of the wooden chairs to steady herself. She forced her face into a smile, but just couldn't make any sort of sound come out of her mouth.

'Who was that?' Sunny asked, handing Kitty her latte.

As Kitty reached for the cup, she noticed her hands were shaking. Some of the milk froth bubbled out of the hole in the lid.

'She lives next door to my gran,' she told Hannah.

'Cool hair,' Hannah said, watching Dylan leave.

Kitty turned to watch Dylan leave too. She wanted to go after her. No, she wished she was leaving with her. She wished she was with her, full stop. Which was ridiculous, since she'd never even spoken to her. But at least now Dylan had spoken to her. Dylan had spoken to her!

'I . . . need to go to the loo,' Kitty said, handing her latte back to Sunny.

'Now?' Hannah said. 'Can't you wait till school?'

Kitty shook her head and practically shoved past both of them in her eagerness to get to the bathroom.

Once the door was locked and the toilet lid down, Kitty sat and put her head in her hands. She was shaking. She thought she might be sick. Actually, she really did feel like she might be sick. She stood up and lifted the loo seat and waited for the vomit to come. She told herself to breathe in and out slowly until she felt better.

There was a knock at the door and Kitty heard Sunny say, 'Are you okay? We need to get going.'

'Yeah,' Kitty called out. 'Thanks. I'll just be a minute.'

She flushed the loo, turned on the cold tap,

washed her hands and patted some water on her face. She looked at herself in the mirror. That was what Dylan had seen when she'd said hello and Kitty had completely failed to say anything back. She looked okay. She was still a bit red, but not too much. Mostly, she looked terrified. The hand drier wasn't working, so Kitty wiped her hands on some loo roll and went back out to meet her friends.

2

School was total chaos, same as every morning. Kitty, Hannah and Sunny hung around outside the main doors, finishing their drinks and watching some Year 7 boys filming each other planking on the top of the bike lockers.

When the buzzer went – since the renovation, the school had a buzzer rather than a bell – the three of them squeezed their takeaway cups into the almost-overflowing bin and went inside.

Once they were through the main doors, people seemed to be coming at them from every direction. (The Head had tried to set up a one-way system when the new building first opened, but no one took any notice.) They had to stop dead when a flustered-looking girl dropped her bag, and pens and books skittered across the polished floor.

'Whoa there!' someone said, crashing into the back of them.

'Sorry,' Kitty said, looking over her shoulder. It was Sam. Again. He grinned at her.

'Were you following us, Sam?' Sunny said, smiling. 'I saw you in Starbucks.'

'Yep. You know I have to keep an eye on you,' Sam said. His tie was already skew-whiff, even though they'd only just arrived at school. 'Don't know what you could be smuggling under that headscarf.'

Sunny grinned. 'I'll never tell.'

The buzzer went again and Sam said, 'Gotta go! Can't be late again – I'm on a yellow card,' and darted around the pencil hazard.

'Er, racist much?' Hannah said.

Sunny shook her head. 'He's talking about when Oliver asked what would happen if I took it off. My scarf, I mean. Didn't I tell you? It was in Sociology.'

'What did he think would happen?' Kitty said, frowning. They set off walking again, the stationery all having been picked up and packed away, the girl almost in tears.

'*What happens if you take it off?*' Sunny mimicked. '*Does your head explode or something?*'

'Oh my god,' Hannah said.

'Right?' Sunny said. 'Sam suggested I pull it off and shout "BANG!"' She grinned. 'He's all right.'

'He fancies Kitty,' Hannah said.

'He doesn't!' Kitty rolled her eyes. She wished Hannah would stop going on about it. She'd already told her she wasn't interested, so what was the point?

'Which Oliver said that about your scarf?' Hannah asked Sunny, as they walked up the curved staircase to their Year 9 cloakroom pod.

'Oliver Collins,' Sunny said. 'Why?'

'I was just thinking,' Hannah said. 'Maybe he likes you. Maybe that's his version of pulling the hair of a girl he fancies. He can't get at your hair, so . . .'

'Ugh, I hope not,' Sunny said. 'He picks his nose with the arm of his glasses.'

'Why are you trying to fix us both up?' Kitty asked Hannah. She wondered sometimes if Hannah made these comments to remind her and Sunny that they'd never had a boyfriend, unlike Hannah.

Hannah laughed. 'I'm not. I just think you should know if someone's interested.'

'But I'm not interested in Sam and Sunny's not interested in Oliver,' Kitty said. 'Are you, Sun?'

Sunny shook her head. 'Definitely not. And even if I was, I can't go out with him or anything.'

Sunny's parents wouldn't let her have a boyfriend while she was still at high school. Sunny told them that she was happy to go along with that until she met someone she actually liked, but everyone knew she didn't mean it really. Her parents could be strict, but she would never do anything to upset them.

By the time the three of them had put their coats and bags in their lockers, the buzzer had gone and they had to go back downstairs again for registration.

'I'm just going to go to the loo,' Hannah said at the bottom of the stairs.

'Should've gone in Starbucks,' Sunny said.

They were cutting through the open-plan library in the light-filled foyer when Hannah stopped and said, 'It doesn't matter. I'll go after.'

'What's up?' Kitty said. But when she looked past Hannah, she saw the reason she'd stopped – Hannah's ex-boyfriend Louis with his new girlfriend, Mackenzie. They were leaning against the wall next to the loo, their heads close together, his hand on her bum.

'It's way too early for that.' Hannah spun round and headed back towards the hall without even looking at Kitty or Sunny.

'I've got something very interesting to tell you about this morning,' the Head, Mrs Savage, said.

'That makes a nice change,' Hannah muttered.

She wasn't wrong, Kitty thought. The assembly had already lasted twenty minutes and most of it had been about a new recycling scheme, the rock-climbing club going on some outing and how if everyone didn't start putting their trays on the trolleys in the canteen, instead of leaving them lying around 'like animals', there'd be a letter going home to parents.

'I didn't know animals ate off trays,' Hannah whispered.

Kitty giggled and shushed her.

'The St Margaret's tourist board has asked me to tell you about a competition they're running for Year 9 and above,' Mrs Savage said.

There was muttering from the lower years and, next to Kitty, Hannah stifled a yawn.

'They are planning a "relaunch and rebrand" of the town,' the Head continued. 'What they want is a short film to run as part of a wider campaign that will focus on the town as a tourist destination and a . . . funky place to live.'

There was quite a lot of sniggering at the word 'funky' and Mrs Savage almost looked embarrassed, but recovered quickly.

'There are prizes.' She unfolded a leaflet she had

in her hand and held it up, even though it was much too small for anyone to really see. 'The winning film will become part of the campaign, of course, but the winning film-makers will go on a film-making course in London. There will also be the inevitable laptops and iPads and whatnot.'

Sunny nudged Kitty and whispered, 'We should do that!'

Kitty shook her head. Those kinds of things always turned out to be too much trouble.

'Staff members will be on hand to help and of course the school will assist with resources,' Mrs Savage said. 'It's an excellent opportunity. I am sure that at least some of you can take a few days out of your busy texting schedule to do something that could perhaps change the course of your life.'

3

'I think we should do it,' Sunny said, shoving the leaflet across the table to Kitty.

'When did you get that?' Kitty asked, turning the leaflet the right way round. It featured a photo of an old-fashioned film camera – one with a reel – projecting a photo of St Margaret's on to a blue sky.

'I went to the media room after Art.'

Even though it was halfway through summer term, it was raining, so they stayed inside in one of the building's new 'social areas' – a round alcove off the main corridor. The steamed-up, floor-to-ceiling windows facing the yard had been decorated with various initials, smiley faces and the inevitable boy-parts.

'But why?' Kitty said. 'None of us knows anything about film-making.'

'No, but you take fantastic photos,' Sunny told her.

Kitty shook her head. 'Taking photos isn't the same as making films.'

'It's in the same area,' Hannah said.

'And the school will lend us the equipment,' Sunny said. 'Ms Guyomar said. She'll help with editing and music and if we need costumes or anything we can get them from Miss Avison.'

'Why would we need costumes?' Kitty said. 'We're not going to be in it.'

'We could be in it,' Sunny said. 'Maybe it'll go viral and we'll be famous.'

Kitty shuddered. 'I don't want to be famous. Everyone looking at you and knowing personal stuff about you? No thanks.'

'It's not *TOWIE*,' Sunny said. 'It's just a local film. I promise you won't get papped.' She grinned at Kitty.

'I'm with Kitty,' Hannah said and flicked the leaflet back to Sunny. 'We're not going to do it.'

'But why?' Sunny said.

'It'd take up loads of time,' Kitty said. 'We'd end up with Ms Guyomar or Mrs Savage on at us about it all the time. They'd probably end up wanting to show it to the whole school and it'd just be humiliating.'

'Zactly,' Hannah said.

Sunny held the leaflet up in front of her face. 'Wouldn't it be brilliant to go on the course? You could see Tom!'

Kitty frowned. She really would love the chance to see her brother, Tom. He was at uni in London, but rarely had enough money to get him home for a visit.

'That's for the winner,' Kitty said. 'What makes you think we could win?'

'A positive mental attitude,' Sunny said, grinning. 'Come on. It'll be fun.'

'You've got a weird idea of fun,' Kitty said. She took the leaflet off Sunny again and scanned it. It did sound like a good opportunity. The winning film would be used by the tourist board to promote the town. The winner was going to be announced at a special presentation. And there was a £5,000 prize.

'Five grand?' Kitty said. 'Mrs Savage didn't mention that.'

'No, she didn't,' Sunny said. 'But it says it right . . . here.' She tapped the leaflet with her longest fingernail.

Kitty looked at Hannah, who shrugged. 'We'd have to make sure *we* get the money, not the school. Knowing Savage, she'll want it for more tray trolleys or something.'

'Yeah,' Kitty said. 'But I could really do with five grand. A third of five grand, I mean.'

'Yep,' Sunny nodded. 'You need the money, I want it for uni –'

'That's years off, Sunny,' Kitty said. 'I can't believe you're even thinking about it.'

'I have to think about it. My parents talk about it all the time. Mum actually sent off for some prospectus things, just "to give you an idea".' She did air quotes.

Hannah shrugged. 'At least she's interested. Mum barely speaks to me any more. She just leaves angry notes for me on the fridge.'

'She's still working all the time?' Kitty asked.

Hannah nodded. 'She's got a really big case on. She can't tell me anything about it except that it's incredibly important. Not more important than me, obviously. That would be a terrible thing to say . . .' She pulled a sarcastic face. 'But, you know, she's never home, so . . . Actually, I wouldn't mind my own "important project". That way I've got a good reason not to do all her crap for her.'

'So that's decided it then,' Sunny said. 'We'll go and see Guyomar and get the stuff. I'll go to the library and get some books about film-making and we'll make a film that'll blow their minds and solve all our problems!'

Kitty laughed. 'We can find out more about it anyway.'

'Do you want to go at lunch?' Sunny asked. 'It'll have to be first thing because I've got prayers at quarter to.'

'No, I want lunch at lunch,' Hannah said. 'Can we go later?'

'Fine,' Sunny said. 'I'll go to the library and do some research and then we can see Ms Guyomar before we go home.'

The buzzer went and they grabbed their bags and headed off to their lessons, leaving the leaflet on the table.

Since the renovation, the media lab was the coolest place in the school by far. Kitty loved going in there because she could pretend she was at some quirky London art college instead of a school five minutes' walk from her house. One whole wall was glass, which overlooked the new 'recreation areas' and every desk had a Mac – some with computer keyboards and some with musical keyboards. A flatscreen TV was set into the wall, showing information and updates about the school intercut with film of school projects, like the dance show and the art exhibition Year 11 had done in the town hall.

'So you decided to do it!' Ms Guyomar said, beaming at Sunny.

'We're going to try,' Kitty said.

'That's all you can do,' Ms Guyomar said, pushing

her curly black hair back from her face. 'Do your best. Be yourselves. Great things will happen.'

'Is anyone else doing it?' Sunny asked.

'A few people have asked me about it, but most of the older students say they haven't got time. Too many exams, et cetera. Such a shame. It's so important to do something creative. Do any of you have a camera?'

They shook their heads.

Ms Guyomar pulled a set of keys out of her bag. 'Wait here. I'll get you a good one.'

As soon as the teacher left the room, Hannah clicked the mouse on one of the computers and the screen sprung to life to show the internet – on someone's Facebook page.

Kitty rolled her eyes. 'Leave it alone, Hannah.'

'What kind of an idiot would leave their Facebook open on a school computer?' Hannah asked. 'Oh, that kind of idiot.'

It was Mackenzie's page. Her profile photo was mostly her doing the pouty duckface thing, but you could just see Louis on the edge of the shot: one eye and the corner of his smiling mouth.

'I feel like writing something just to teach her a lesson,' Hannah said.

'About internet safety?' Sunny said, faux-innocently, taking her new notebook out of her bag.

'No, no,' Kitty said. 'Step away from the computer – it's not worth it.'

'Spoilsport,' Hannah said.

'How does this one look?' Ms Guyomar said, coming back into the room holding a tiny black camera. Kitty and Sunny went to look while Hannah closed Mackenzie's page.

Ms Guyomar spent the next five minutes showing the girls how to use the camera, while Sunny made notes, neither of which were really necessary, since it could have been summed up as: Press this button, look at this screen and make sure there's a memory card in it.

'It's not our best camera,' Ms Guyomar said. 'I'm afraid you were beaten to that one –'

'Who by?' Sunny said.

'Oh,' the teacher frowned. 'Mackenzie Clarke. Amber Moran and . . . a boy I don't know.'

'Louis Stevens,' Hannah said.

'Yes!' Ms Guyomar said, looking delighted. 'Louis Stevens.'

'They're entering the competition too?' Kitty asked.

Ms Guyomar nodded. 'They are. They came to see me at lunchtime, so I'm afraid they got the top-of-the-range stuff.'

'Great,' Sunny said. 'Thanks.'

'I'm not doing it,' Hannah said as soon as they left the classroom.

'I knew you were going to say that,' Kitty said. 'But we won't have to do anything with them –'

'You know what Savage is like,' Hannah said. 'She's all about teamwork and collaboration. And I'm not spending any time with Louis or Mackenzie.'

'We won't have to spend time with them,' Sunny said. 'We'll be doing our projects independently. We can make sure they're not there when we see Ms Guyomar. Just pretend he's not involved. And think of the money. Or annoying your mum. Whatever works.'

Hannah shook her head. 'I don't know. I just want to keep away from him, you know?'

'You don't still like him?' Kitty asked.

Hannah had gone out with Louis for a few months before she'd found out he was cheating on her with Mackenzie. She said she wasn't bothered, but Kitty thought she was more upset than she let on. Hannah never liked to admit to being bothered by anything.

'God, no,' Hannah said. 'But Mackenzie likes to shove it in my face anyway. And that Amber cow's just as bad – she's like Mackenzie's Mini-Me.'

'So don't you want to beat them?' Sunny said.

Hannah stopped walking and frowned. 'I want to batter them.'

'I meant in the competition . . .' Sunny said.

Hannah almost smiled. 'Me too. Sort of.'

'Think how angry Mackenzie will be if we win,' Sunny said.

'And think how much she'll gloat if we lose,' Hannah said.

'So we'd better not lose,' Kitty said.

4

Coming home from school used to be Kitty's favourite part of the day. It wasn't that she didn't like school – it was okay, especially since the renovation, and she loved her friends – but she just loved coming home. Her mum would be back from work. She was a teacher and for the last couple of years, until she got ill, she'd actually been working at Grace's school. She'd already be making dinner, but she'd have a snack ready for Kitty and Grace, and Grace would go and watch CBBC while Kitty would stay in the kitchen and tell her mum all about her day.

Today, by the time she'd kicked off her school shoes in the hall, her dad was on his way back out to work.

'Good day?' he asked, kissing the top of her head as he passed her.

'Yeah, actually,' Kitty said.

'Pop up and see your mum in a bit. She's been

looking forward to seeing you. Grace is watching telly. I'll be back for dinner – can you make it?'

Kitty nodded.

'Be good,' he said.

'Be careful,' she said, closing the front door behind him.

Kitty took Grace a glass of milk and some biscuits, then went upstairs to see her mum. She hated that she felt nervous going into her parents' bedroom these days. They used to all pile in bed together on weekend mornings, and sometimes she, Grace and their mum would watch a film there together when their dad was on lates. But now it was Mum's room and they didn't like to disturb her. She wondered if Dad even felt weird about it.

Kitty pushed open the bedroom door. The room was in darkness and smelled a bit musty and sour – the way rooms do when someone's been shut up in them all day.

'Mum?' Kitty whispered.

She almost tiptoed across the room. Her mum was fast asleep, frowning slightly, a John Grisham book face down on the pillow next to her.

Kitty felt relieved. And then guilty for feeling relieved.

As she walked back downstairs her phone buzzed in her pocket. A message from Sunny.

High concept: car chase along the prom.

Kitty sat down on the stairs and replied.

None of us can drive.

By the time she'd got to the kitchen, there was another message.

Low concept: sitting in car pretending to drive.

Kitty laughed out loud and replied, *Keep thinking.*

'Is that your homework?' Grace said.

Kitty had been concentrating hard on *A Midsummer Night's Dream* and felt almost dreamy herself. She blinked at her sister. 'Yeah.'

'Is it boring?' Grace said.

'It's . . . yeah, a bit. It's just hard. You have to really concentrate.'

'Oh. Sorry.' Grace picked at the corner of the *101 Dalmatians* table mat she'd had since she was a toddler.

'It's okay,' Kitty said. 'I probably need to start making tea anyway.'

Kitty got up and crossed the room to the kitchen, opening the top cupboard for the pasta. There wasn't much there. There wasn't much of anything there. That was something else that had changed.

Grace followed her.

'Are you okay?' Kitty asked over her shoulder as she filled a pan with water from the tap. 'Keep away from the cooker.'

'I was just thinking about Mum,' Grace said.

Kitty put the pan on the hob and turned to look at her sister.

'Have you been up to see her?'

Grace shook her head. 'I just wanted to . . . I know Dad said we shouldn't Google it. But I just want to know some things.'

'Okay.'

'Is it . . . is Mum going to die?'

Kitty's breath caught painfully behind her ribs.

'I think . . . Do you want to go and sit down?'

Her sister shook her head.

'Okay.' She leaned back against the sink. 'I think . . . maybe sooner than she would have done? But not definitely. It's not a terminal disease, I mean. It's not like cancer or something. She can live with it.'

Grace nodded, still frowning. 'And is it . . . It's not contagious?'

Kitty shook her head. 'No! It's not contagious. You know that, Gracie. Dad said.'

'That's the wrong word. I don't mean can we catch

it. I mean, will me and you get it? Are we more likely to get it cos Mum's got it?'

Kitty scuffed at a torn bit of lino with her foot. 'I don't know, Gracie. Okay? I'll find out. Don't look it up.'

'I won't,' Grace said. 'I couldn't. I don't even know how to spell it. I keep getting the name wrong.'

Kitty didn't tell her she could Google 'MS'. She'd rather Grace didn't know any more about multiple sclerosis than she absolutely had to. She wished none of them needed to know anything about it at all.

'Okay?' Kitty said.

'Okay,' Grace said. She spat out the bit of hair she'd been chewing. 'How long's tea going to be? I'm starving.'

'You've done us proud here, Kitty,' her dad said, reaching across the table for some garlic bread.

Kitty smiled. Her dad always tried to make her feel better even though she pretty much always made spaghetti bolognese. They'd made it at school and it was one of the only things that hadn't come out completely terrible.

'It looks really good, Kitty,' her mum said. She was in her usual seat – the seat she always used to sit in to read and drink coffee and talk to her friends on the house phone – but she was in a dressing gown and looked tired and drained.

'Smells good too,' Kitty's dad said. 'Tuck in!'

After such a build-up, Kitty was relieved to find the spag bol did actually taste really good. She hadn't realised she was so hungry, so she shovelled it in. The rest of her family seemed to be doing the same and, as long as she only looked at her mum out of the corner of her eye, she could pretend that everything was fine.

Dad talked while he ate. He told them about the passengers he'd had in his cab – the woman who left her mobile on the seat and actually ran after the car to get it back, and a man who asked how much it would be for a journey that would take two hours and then admitted he only had a tenner. Grace chattered about school – one of her friends had been sick in the playground at lunchtime, there was going to be a trip to a textiles museum in Lancashire. Kitty told them about the film project. Her mum didn't talk much, but she ate her garlic bread and smiled and laughed at Dad's stupid jokes.

Kitty had just been thinking it was the best meal they'd had together for ages, when she realised something was wrong. With her mum. For a few seconds she couldn't make herself look – she was enjoying herself and didn't want it to end. But she could hear her mum sighing and sort of huffing and she knew she couldn't ignore it any longer.

'What's wrong?' she said.

Her dad looked up from his spaghetti. He'd never been good at picking it up so usually ended up with his face practically in his bowl.

'I can't . . .' Kitty's mum said, clasping her hands together. 'I can't pick the spaghetti up.'

She picked her fork up again, put it on the edge of the bowl and tried to twirl it, but it didn't move.

'I feel like my fingers are moving, but they're not,' she said.

'Can you do it with the other hand?' Grace asked.

They were all staring.

Mum shook her head. 'I've never been able to do it with my other hand. It doesn't matter. I'll just scoop them up, like your dad does.'

'It's much easier,' he said, smiling. 'I recommend it.'

They all ate some more, but the atmosphere had changed. Dad tried to start a few more conversations, but it had all gone wrong. Kitty hated seeing her mum so vulnerable. She was supposed to be the grown-up.

It wasn't fair. Kitty felt tears burning behind her eyes. She blinked them away.

'Is there pudding?' Grace said hopefully as soon as the three of them had finished and Mum had given up.

'There's ice cream,' Kitty said, but she knew she wasn't going to have any. Her stomach felt icy enough already.

'Not for me, thanks,' Mum said.

Kitty felt anger bubbling up inside her. She knew none of this was her mum's fault. But she was so angry she wanted to shout. Or knock over the table. She stood up quickly, her chair falling back and hitting the wall.

'I don't want any either,' she said. 'I've got to go out.'

'Where?' her mum said, looking confused. 'What time is it?'

'I've got to go to Hannah's. I left my bag there and I've got homework.'

'Well, make sure you come straight back,' her dad said.

'I will,' Kitty said. She grabbed her jacket and, without looking at anyone, walked straight out of the door.

5

Wiping her wet face with the backs of her hands, Kitty almost ran down to the prom and climbed over the railings to drop down to the beach. She pulled off her Converse and headed straight to the water's edge. The water was absolutely freezing, but it felt good too – it concentrated all her thoughts to the iciness of her feet and the smooth stones under her toes. She turned towards the park and walked along the sand, kicking at the water, inhaling the seaweed smell she'd grown up with, and going over what had just happened. She knew it was unreasonable. She knew her mum would be upset. Probably her dad too. And Grace. But she was just so sick of her mum's illness ruining everything, even meals.

Kitty picked up a rock and rubbed it with her thumb. It was cold and wet and smooth and fitted perfectly in the palm of her hand. Turning back towards the river, she threw it overarm into the water. It gave a satisfying splash. Kitty watched the ripples spreading out, out, out, and wondered how far they would go. Would they just keep on going, even when she couldn't see them? She picked up another rock and tried to throw it further. Soon, she was bending, throwing, watching for the splash, bending, throwing . . . She was starting to pant and her arm muscles were burning, but she wasn't thinking about her mum or anything else – she was totally immersed in beating her last throw and making a bigger splash. When she finally stopped, she found she was laughing out loud. She was amazed at how much better she felt. The heavy feeling in her stomach – which had felt like one of the stones she'd just been throwing had settled there – had gone. She tipped her head back to the sky and took a deep breath.

'Are you okay?'

Kitty gave a little shriek and turned towards the voice. Dylan was sitting on the prom railings, grinning down at her.

'You scared me!' Kitty said. She licked her lips and tasted salt.

'Sorry,' Dylan said. She launched herself off the railings, making the two-metre drop to the sand look easy. Kitty always turned round and dangled until her feet were only about half a metre off the ground.

'What are you doing here?' Kitty asked. She could feel her heart pounding. It felt like it was leaping out of her chest, like in a cartoon.

'I was walking home and I saw you trying to beat the sea up, so I stopped to watch.' Dylan smiled and pushed her fringe back out of her eyes.

'You were at school late?'

Dylan nodded. 'Yeah. Meeting about this film competition for the local council.'

'I'm doing that!' Kitty said.

Dylan grinned. 'Cool. I'm not though. I thought about it, but I decided it would take up too much time.'

'Oh.' Kitty was surprised at how disappointed she felt. Even though the schools were working on their films individually, maybe there'd be meetings or something where she could have seen Dylan. Even if there weren't, she still liked the idea of them having something in common, both working on the same thing.

'Do you go to Whiteacre?' Kitty asked, bending down and picking up a shell.

Whiteacre was a really small school behind the park. The students didn't wear uniform and they didn't have a curriculum, but were free to follow their own interests.

Dylan nodded. 'You?'

'Quarry Mount.' Kitty realised there was something still alive in the shell so dropped it back on the sand. 'What's Whiteacre like?'

'I love it,' Dylan said. 'I've not been there long, but it's much better than my old school.' She smiled at Kitty. 'Have you got big plans? For the competition?'

'So far we've just got notes in my friend Sunny's exercise book.' Kitty smiled back. 'But she did get a new one specially.'

Dylan laughed out loud. She had one of those laughs that kind of bursts out with no introduction. Kitty felt proud of herself. Last time she'd seen Dylan she hadn't even been able to speak. And now she'd made her laugh.

'You can't argue with new stationery,' Dylan said.

They looked at each other. Dylan didn't have the silver scarf around her hair any more. Kitty wondered where it was. She tried to think of something to say, but her mind was as blank as Sunny's exercise book.

'So . . . are you okay?' Dylan asked. She nodded towards the water.

'Oh!' Kitty blushed. 'Yeah. I just . . . I was a bit

annoyed and I came out for a walk and . . . did that. And now I feel much better.'

'When I was little, if I had a tantrum, my dad used to get me to punch the sofa cushions. It always made me feel better.'

Kitty smiled again. 'I'll try that sometime.'

'These days he's the one I want to punch, so it was a good job he did.' Dylan bent and picked up one of the rocks.

Kitty opened and closed her mouth. She wasn't sure what she should say to that.

'Sorry,' Dylan said. 'My dad . . . lots of drama there. You don't need to know.' She threw the rock, but underarm so it didn't travel very far. A few flecks of water splashed the bottom of her legs and she stepped back, closer to Kitty.

Kitty was still lost for words. Her brain was in a frenzy of trying to find something to say, but she just wasn't coming up with anything. Dylan was going to think she was a complete idiot.

'I'd better go,' Dylan said, smiling at her. 'I don't want to miss the ferry.'

'I'll walk with you!' Kitty said. The relief of finally having something to say made it come out slightly too loud. 'I live that way.'

She didn't – she lived in the opposite direction entirely. But she wanted to spend more time with Dylan. She couldn't quite believe she'd just lied about where she lived, but she didn't want to go home yet. And it was only a little lie.

'Cool,' Dylan said.

They walked along the beach as far as the stone steps, then climbed to the prom, holding the handrail because the steps were slippery with bright green moss. At the top of the steps, Kitty sat down and rubbed her sandy feet against her jeans before tugging her Converse back on. She didn't bother tying the laces, she just tucked them inside – she didn't want Dylan to go without her.

'I love those,' Dylan said when she stood up. 'I had a red pair, but they got ruined when I tried to jump over a muddy puddle and didn't quite make it. Came out with one shoe on and one off.'

Kitty laughed, but her stomach fluttered with nerves as they passed the park. What if Hannah or Sunny was there? She was pretty sure they wouldn't be. They wouldn't go without her. And it's not as if she was doing anything. She was just walking, with a girl. But if Hannah or Sunny saw them, she'd have to introduce them to Dylan and they'd want to know who she was and how they'd met and she just didn't want that. Not yet.

She looked quickly through the railings. Some Year 10 boys were playing football in front of the bandstand, but she didn't know them well enough to acknowledge them. Or for them to notice her. A couple was sitting on the bench just inside the gates – the man was looking at his phone, but the woman had her legs slung over his, her hand inside his shirt. He put his phone down and kissed her. Kitty looked away.

What would it be like if she and Dylan were going out? What would it be like walking along here with her . . . girlfriend? Her stomach leaped like when her dad drove too fast over a hill to make her laugh. She wasn't entirely sure whether it was a good feeling. What would people think if they saw them together? How would it feel to know that people were looking at them? She hated the idea that people might look at her and be thinking about her and Dylan together. She glanced at Dylan. Somehow she didn't think Dylan would care about that kind of thing.

Kitty mentally slapped herself. She was being ridiculous. She barely knew Dylan anyway and, since she couldn't seem to speak around her, Dylan probably thought she was a total weirdo.

Dylan looked over at her and smiled, and Kitty's stomach fluttered. She had to say something – maybe she could ask her about school – but just as she opened her mouth to speak, Dylan said, 'This is going to sound really weird . . . but I really like your gran.'

Kitty laughed. 'No, that's not weird. Everyone does.'

'She's been so nice to us since we moved. My mum was worried about moving to a new area and everything. Not knowing anyone? But your gran –'

'Knows everyone,' Kitty interrupted.

'Yeah. She's got Mum involved in all sorts of mad stuff.'

'The Women's Institute.'

'Yeah, and some sponsored crochet thing. Our house is full of wool and little patterned triangles, you know?' Dylan made a triangle with her fingers and Kitty noticed that her silver nail varnish was chipped. More than chipped – half of each short nail was bare.

'They're trying to make the biggest bunting . . .' Kitty said.

'But . . . why?'

Kitty laughed. 'No idea. It was yarn-bombing last year. They knitted jumpers for all the trees in the street.'

'She's so cool though,' Dylan said. 'Careful!'

Kitty gasped as Dylan grabbed her arm.

'Sorry,' Dylan said, pulling a face. 'I thought you were going to step in some –'

'Oh! Yeah. Sorry,' Kitty said, glancing back at the pile of dog muck she'd narrowly avoided. Her arm was tingling where Dylan had grabbed it and her face felt hot.

'Sorry, I've forgotten what we were talking about,' she said.

'Your gran,' Dylan said. 'She's great.'

'Yeah,' Kitty said. 'She is.'

Her gran was cool, she knew, and she was thrilled that Dylan thought so too.

'Next time you're over we should hang out,' Dylan said. 'Your gran's being saying for ages that she thought we'd get on.'

Kitty blushed. Was that why Dylan was talking to her? Because her gran had asked her to? She felt like she should probably say no – she didn't want Dylan to feel like she had to be nice to her. But she wanted to spend more time with her, Gran or no Gran. So she said, 'That'd be cool.'

They crossed the road to the ferry terminal and Kitty glanced up at the clock on the front of the huge stone building. Her parents would be expecting her home by now.

Dylan grinned at her. 'Thanks for walking me. Where do you live?'

'Just up there,' Kitty said, waving vaguely at the nearest street.

'Cool.' Dylan said. She took a step closer as if she was maybe going for a hug and Kitty stepped backwards in fright.

Dylan stopped and grinned. 'See you.'

'Bye.'

Dylan headed down the ramp, turning once to wave. Kitty watched her go until she went through the turnstile and disappeared on to the boat. She wanted to kick herself. Actually properly kick herself. Why had she freaked at the thought of a hug? Dylan was going to think she was a complete loser.

Just to be on the safe side, Kitty set off up the road she'd pointed to. Clearly she *was* a loser, walking up a random road, pretending she lived there. What if Dylan had asked to come to her house? She stopped just as the road curved – close enough that she could see the river, but too far for Dylan to see her.

Then, once the ferry had gone, she turned back down to the prom towards home.

6

After school the next day, Kitty, Hannah and Sunny headed for the park. Kitty's dad wasn't working until later so she wanted to take advantage of being with her friends, in the sun.

As they walked along the prom, she started worrying that they might bump into Dylan. She was so pathetic around her that Hannah and Sunny would guess she liked her. Wouldn't they? Hannah probably would. She was always looking out for that kind of thing. And she didn't want Hannah teasing her about it. Even if she was only messing. Or maybe they wouldn't think any such thing. Maybe the last thing they'd think was that she'd be interested in a girl. She really had no idea. It was so much easier to keep them separate. For as long as possible.

They turned into the park and headed up the path towards the bandstand. Some of the boys from their school were already playing football – their ties off and shirts undone. Someone wolf-whistled and Hannah shouted, 'Sexist pigs!' The boys all laughed.

'That was Sam,' Sunny said, waggling her eyebrows at Kitty.

'Oh don't you start!' Kitty said. 'Why are you both so convinced he likes me? I don't think I've ever even had a conversation with him!'

'I don't think he's interested in your conversation,' Hannah said, nudging Kitty's arm.

Kitty laughed, but her stomach was churning. This was the kind of thing that would change if she told the girls about Dylan. They'd always teased each other about boys, even in primary school when Josh Atkins, who Hannah was mad about, fainted when he saw a skull on the school trip to the Natural History Museum. And when Sunny got sent to the head for hitting Harrison Blake when he tried to kiss her in PE.

They climbed the steps to the bandstand and sat on the edge, swinging their legs and kicking their heels against the base.

Kitty looked across the park. Dogs were running everywhere and she could hear children shrieking at the kids' playground near the café. Hannah was looking at her phone, which hadn't left her hand since they'd come out of school.

'So have you had any ideas for the film?' Sunny said, fiddling with her headscarf. 'I think we need to come up with something really fun. Fun to watch, I mean. I saw these tourist info films on YouTube and they were so boring – you could tell they'd been made by the council. I want to make something people will watch even if they would never think of coming here.'

'You want it to go viral?' Hannah said.

Sunny nodded as she refastened one of the sparkly clips that held her hijab in place.

'You're ambitious, Sun, I'll give you that.'

'I haven't really thought of anything though . . .' Sunny said.

'Me neither,' Kitty said.

'I was talking to my nan about it.' Hannah put her hand up to her forehead to shield her eyes from the sun, her phone still in it. 'And she kept going on about how great St Margaret's used to be, right? She was talking about the outdoor pool and the fair and the ballroom and the zoo.'

'There was a zoo?' Kitty said. 'Wow!'

'Yeah! I didn't know that either. Apparently they used to walk the elephants on the beach. That was when she was a little girl. She kept saying, "I don't know what you young ones do now. It doesn't seem like there's much fun . . ."'

'Isn't your nan about fifty?' Sunny said.

'No, that's my gran! This is my nan. She's eighty, I think.'

'Right,' Sunny said.

'So I told her a few places – you know, the Bee, the lighthouse, the pier. I told her the Lanes are still cool and the park. So what I thought was we could get some old film – or photos even – of what it used to be like here and compare it with what it's like now. What do you think?'

Kitty and Sunny stared at her.

'But . . . wasn't it nicer before?' Kitty asked.

Hannah rolled her eyes. 'We'll film all the good stuff now. We'll make it look really cool. It'd be like . . . you don't know what you've been missing. You know?'

'I like it,' Kitty said. 'I'm going to my gran's tomorrow. I can ask her about it too.'

'Sounds good,' Sunny agreed.

'We'd have a photo of the lighthouse when it was an actual lighthouse,' Hannah said, 'and then film of it now it's a bar, lit up at night, with the fairy lights and everything.'

'That could work,' Kitty said. 'So we'd have something for older people who are into history and stuff, and then something for younger people too.'

'St Margaret's: The Best of Both Worlds!' Sunny said.

'I love it,' Kitty said. 'And we don't even have to be in it.'

'Perfect,' Hannah grinned.

The sun was dazzling them, so they jumped down from the bandstand and walked through the rose garden and up the hill to the café. Kitty thought about how many times they'd done this over the years. It must have been hundreds. She was surprised they hadn't worn their own path.

'Remember that time we came here,' Kitty said, 'and we—'

'I was just thinking about that!' Hannah said. 'When we stayed after dark?'

'You two did,' Sunny said, walking around the opposite side of one of the flower beds. 'I went home.'

'That's because you're a good girl,' Hannah said, smiling at her.

It was towards the end of Year 6, when they'd been visiting high schools and thinking about what it would be like not to be at primary any more. At the time, they weren't sure if they'd all be going to the same secondary, so they were spending even more time together than usual. Just in case.

'Oh my god – when your dad lit that barbecue!' Hannah said.

Sunny laughed. 'Mum still talks about that.'

Sunny's dad had brought a proper barbecue to the park, but when he tried to light it, flames shot out and people screamed. Sunny's mum had yelled at him until he'd put the lid back on it and taken it home.

'Have you still got it?' Kitty asked Sunny.

'I think Mum gave it away that day! She was scared Dad would burn the house down.'

'You stayed after they left though,' Kitty said. 'Didn't you?'

'Not long,' Sunny said. 'I think I stayed a bit longer than I should have done, but not like you two.'

It had been one of those perfect early summer days – hot, but with a cool breeze off the river, people picnicking all over the park. A brass band was playing songs from musicals on the bandstand and Hannah had some money so she and Kitty kept going back to the café for drinks and crisps and ice creams.

'I bet it wasn't even that late,' Hannah said, as

they came out of the rose garden and followed the concrete path.

'It wasn't!' Kitty said. 'It was eight o'clock!'

'Yeah, but they didn't know where you were,' Sunny said. 'So you know why they were freaking out.'

'I can still picture my mum's face as she came down the hill,' Hannah said. 'Like the Hulk. She wouldn't even notice now.'

'Mine were more upset than angry, I think,' Kitty said. 'Although by the time we got home, they were thinking up punishments.'

'It was worth it though,' Hannah said.

Kitty laughed. 'It totally was.'

'You two have all the fun,' Sunny said, squeezing between them.

'Will you go and get the drinks?' Hannah said, as they walked in a wide arc around some dogs tied up to the railings outside. 'I'm just going to the loo.'

Hannah disappeared around the corner of the building – the café didn't have its own loo so customers had to use the park's public toilets – and Kitty went inside to get the drinks. As soon as she walked in, she saw Mackenzie and Amber, and stifled a groan. She ignored them as she queued, but once she'd got the drinks and was heading back towards the door, Mackenzie said, 'Where's your friend?'

Kitty thought about pretending she didn't realise Mackenzie was talking to her, but that was more trouble than it was worth.

'Which one?' she said.

'The one who thinks it's so hilarious to frape people.' Mackenzie looked at her phone on the table in front of her and then back up at Kitty. 'Tell her if she goes anywhere near my Facebook again, she'll be sorry.'

'I don't know what you're talking about,' Kitty said. 'And I hate that expression – "frape". Writing something on Facebook is nothing like rape.'

'Yeah, whatever,' Mackenzie said, rolling her eyes. 'Oh here's your lesbo friend now.'

Kitty turned back to the door, expecting to see Dylan, but it was just Hannah. There was no way Mackenzie could know anything about her and Dylan – there wasn't anything to know – but Kitty's stomach churned at the thought.

'What's going on?' Hannah said. She looked flushed.

'Nothing,' Kitty said. 'Let's go.' All she could think about was Mackenzie's 'lesbo' comment and what she'd say if she knew that Kitty really did like girls.

'Is she having a go at you?' Hannah asked her.

'No,' Kitty said. 'It's fine. Let's just go.'

'I was telling her to tell you –' Mackenzie started to say, but she didn't finish her sentence, instead she stared out through the door. Kitty looked. It was Louis.

'Come on,' Hannah said to Kitty.

Kitty turned to Mackenzie, who was looking up at Hannah with narrowed eyes. Kitty could see a blotchy red rash starting to crawl up Mackenzie's neck. It happened when she was nervous, Kitty knew. She'd been in the same maths set as Mackenzie last year and that had happened every time she had to answer a question.

'Y'alright?' Louis said, sitting down opposite Mackenzie and Amber and apparently oblivious to the atmosphere between the girls.

'Let's go,' Kitty said again, practically shoving Hannah out of the café.

'What happened?' Hannah asked again.

Kitty kept walking up the hill towards the gate. Her eyes were burning, but she didn't want to cry. She stopped near the kids' playground and turned back to Hannah, who looked surprised, and Sunny, who looked confused.

'Did you put something on her Facebook? Mackenzie's?'

Hannah smiled. 'Oh, is that all? God, you scared me for a minute. It wasn't anything bad!'

'Why do you want to wind her up?' Kitty said. 'Why can't you just ignore her?'

'She stole my boyfriend,' Hannah said. She wasn't smiling any more. She was wearing the 'don't mess with me' face that Kitty had become familiar with over the years. It usually made her back down – she really didn't want to mess with Hannah – but not today. Not after what Mackenzie had said.

'She didn't steal him,' Kitty said. 'He just went off with her. It's as much his fault as it is hers. More actually.'

'Why are you so bothered anyway?' Hannah said.

'Because now she's having a go at me. And probably Sunny too, when she gets a chance. And it's nothing to do with us. It's not fair.'

Hannah rolled her eyes. 'Fine. I'll leave it.'

'Good,' Kitty said. Her pulse had gone back to normal and she'd stopped feeling like she was about to throw up. Now she just felt like she needed to sit down.

'What did she say anyway?' Hannah asked.

'She told me to tell you to keep off her Facebook,' Kitty said. 'And she called you a lesbian.'

Hannah snorted with laughter and rolled her eyes again, as Kitty looked from her to Sunny and back.

'He didn't just go off with her,' Hannah said. She pulled at the leaves on the hedge they were standing next to. 'He went off with her because I wouldn't do stuff. And she would. That's why she called me a lesbian. She must've only just learned the word. She usually pretends to cough "frigid".'

Kitty stared at her friend. 'Seriously?'

'Yeah, she's done it loads of times.'

'No,' Kitty said. 'I mean . . . that's why you and Louis split up?'

'Oh,' Hannah said. 'Yeah.'

'Why didn't you tell us that?' Sunny asked. She linked her arm through Hannah's.

'It's embarrassing.' Hannah shrugged.

'That's awful,' Kitty said. 'You're well rid of him.'

'I know, right?' Hannah hooked her other arm through Kitty's.

The three of them set off walking up the hill.

'I've never seen you like that before, Kits,' Hannah said. 'I like feisty Kitty.'

Kitty tried to smile, but she still felt wobbly. 'I don't.'

7

Kitty got off the train and walked up the stairs rather than wait for the lift. The stairs were old, with curly iron bannisters, and the steps dipped a bit in the middle where people had walked on them over the years. She'd always loved the steps – they made her think about how many people had come through this station and made her wonder where they were going and what they were doing – but today she couldn't get up them quickly enough.

She'd only started being allowed to come over to her gran's on her own after her fourteenth birthday, but it had soon become one of her favourite things to do. She could have got the ferry – like Dylan had – but then she'd have had to get a bus and she much preferred the train journey. She loved watching from the window as the train line followed the river before dipping underground. She loved counting off the stations on the map and, just before her gran's stop, getting up to wait, holding on to the handrail near the door. It was the thing that made her feel the most grown up.

Out of the station she turned to walk down the main road, past the parade of shops. She loved these shops too. They were a bit like the parade near her house — both of them had Victorian glass awnings above — but the shops here were a bit funkier, a bit cooler. There was a jazz bar and a deli and a Turkish café with people sitting outside, smoking something from long curly pipes that Kitty's gran told her were called hookahs. She crossed the road to her gran's house and immediately became aware that Dylan could be watching her. She could be sitting at her bedroom window, seeing Kitty approach. Kitty didn't want to look up and find out for sure.

She walked up through her gran's front garden. It was stuffed with bright flowers — all different kinds. Her gran had bought a bag of mixed flower seeds and let Kitty and Grace sprinkle them all around. They'd grown completely randomly, but looked beautiful. People actually knocked on the door to tell her gran how gorgeous it was and it had even been featured in the local newspaper.

Kitty knocked on the red wooden front door and waited to hear her gran call out that she was on her way. But there was no reply. She knocked again and then tried the brass handle, but it was locked. Kitty looked around, as if her gran might be hiding in the garden to surprise her. Then she walked back to the road and looked up and down, in case she was on her way home, but there was no sign of her.

She took out her phone and rang her gran's mobile.

Her gran answered after only a couple of rings with, 'Oh, Kitty!'

'Where are you?' Kitty asked.

'I'm at a meeting. I'm so sorry, I forgot you were coming!'

Kitty walked back to the front door and sat on the step. 'Are you going to be back soon?'

'Oh yes. Hold on a sec . . .'

Kitty heard her gran talking to someone else. Something about a heating rota. And then she said, 'Kitty? I'll be about half an hour, I think.'

'Okay,' Kitty said. She could look in the shops for half an hour. Or go to the library.

'The back door's open,' her gran said down the phone. 'Go and sit in Trevor. There's some magazines in the recycling box.'

'Oh, okay,' Kitty said, standing up and feeling instantly better. 'I'll see you later then.'

'I'll bring us a cake!' Her gran hung up.

Kitty opened the gate next to the front door, walked up a slightly tatty and wobbly path, and opened another gate to her gran's tiny back garden. It was a nice day, so she actually could have just sat out there, but she opened the door to the lean-to – when her gran had bought the house, she couldn't decide whether to call it a lean-to or a sunroom or a conservatory, so in the end she'd just decided to call it 'Trevor' – and stepped inside. Kitty didn't know exactly why, but Trevor was one of her favourite places in the world. The external walls were glass and light shining through the trees made greenish patterns on the tiled floor. The internal wall was the bare brick back wall of the house, broken up by the two huge windows into the lounge. One of them was slightly open and Kitty figured she could probably reach round far enough to open it and climb into the house, but she didn't want to; she wanted to sit in Trevor and read magazines.

She was curled up like a cat in her gran's armchair and halfway through a copy of *Vogue* when she heard the gate open. She actually felt slightly disappointed that her gran was back already. Much as she loved her, she loved sitting by herself and reading *Vogue* in the sunshine. She squinted at the door as it opened.

'Oh! Sorry! I thought you were Molly!' said Dylan.

Kitty opened her mouth to speak, but nothing came out. Again.

'Hey!' Dylan said, smiling.

Kitty was thrilled to notice Dylan looked really pleased to see her. Dylan was probably one of those people who was always really pleased to see everyone, but even so.

'Is Molly in?' Dylan asked.

'Sorry, no,' Kitty said. Her voice sounded slightly strangled. She cleared her throat and tried again. 'She's at a committee meeting, but she won't be long. She should be back in about fifteen minutes, I think.'

'So you're waiting for her and reading *Vogue*?'

Kitty looked at the magazine on her lap. 'Yeah.'

Dylan sat down on the other side of the table and Kitty sucked in her breath. Dylan was going to stay and wait too?

Dylan pulled out another copy of *Vogue* from the pile. 'My nanna wouldn't know *Vogue* if it fell out of a plane on to her head. She doesn't really read magazines at all – except in the hairdresser's, you know – but she really wouldn't understand *Vogue*.'

They both stared at the pile of magazines. Kitty

folded and unfolded the corner of the cover of the one she'd been looking at.

'Your gran was telling me about her job,' Dylan said. 'It sounded amazing.'

Kitty nodded, relieved that Dylan had broken the silence. 'Yeah, she's got some good stories.'

Her gran had worked for years as a personal shopper in one of the big department stores in town and then, after it had closed down, in a little boutique. She was still really into fashion, even though she'd retired a few years ago.

'I love the way she dresses,' Dylan said. 'Does she save clothes for you? For when –' She slapped both hands over her mouth. 'Oh my god. I was going to say for when she dies. How horrible am I?'

Kitty laughed. 'No, she tells me that! Sometimes she gets things out to show me and says, "This'll be yours, after I'm gone."'

Dylan shook her head. 'That's fantastic. I mean, not that she'll be dead, that's terrible, but that she's saving things for you. You're really lucky.'

She smiled at Kitty across the table.

Kitty nodded. She felt lucky.

8

Kitty heard the gate and, for the second time since she'd arrived at her gran's, was disappointed. She didn't want her gran to come home. She wanted to stay here, in her favourite place, talking to this girl she'd had a crush on for ages. This girl who seemed to think she was interesting and worth talking to and spending time with. What if she didn't get the chance again? What if her gran came home and Dylan went away and that was it? Just the thought of it made Kitty feel like all the sun had drained out of the room.

Her gran came in, smiling and full of apologies, with a huge cake box in her hands.

'Oh Dylan, lovely! You'll stay and have some cake, won't you? Of course you will.'

She unlocked the inside door and went in the house for plates and forks and to make a pot of tea.

'You don't mind if I stay?' Dylan asked Kitty.

'Um, yeah . . .' Kitty said. 'I'd rather you left.'

'Oh god, sorry!' Dylan said, starting to get out of her chair.

'I'm joking!' Kitty said. She bit her lip, worried that she'd made a mess of it. She'd barely been able to talk to Dylan before now. Maybe trying to joke with her was too much.

Dylan snorted out a laugh. 'Oh thank god.' She dropped back into her seat. 'I was thinking . . . awkward!'

Kitty felt almost giddy, but she couldn't think of what to say, so she just flicked through the magazine in front of her instead. When she felt a bit calmer, she glanced up at Dylan, only to find Dylan was looking back at her.

'You look like her, you know?' Dylan said, tipping her head on one side. 'Your gran, I mean.'

'People always say that,' Kitty said. 'I can't see it myself.'

'You do,' Dylan said. 'You've got the same bone structure.'

Kitty laughed. 'People usually say "eyes".'

'That too,' Dylan said. 'But it's not just your eyes, it's here too.' She held her own face between her thumb and middle finger to sort of squeeze in her cheeks. It made her lips pout out and Kitty looked at them and then back down at the magazine.

After a couple of minutes of silence, broken only by the flicking of the glossy pages, Dylan told Kitty she wanted to work in fashion.

'As a designer?' Kitty asked.

Kitty didn't know much about fashion. Mainly just what her gran had told her. Hannah was the only one of them to know her Stella McCartney from her Alexander McQueen and the only one of them who could afford anything more expensive than Topshop, although even Topshop was beyond Kitty lately.

Dylan tipped her head to one side. 'Maybe. Or a stylist. I like twisting other people's stuff, you know? Taking something vintage and making it new? I bought this amazing dress from a charity shop − it's pink satin with black lace over the top, but the lace is all torn on the bodice, so I'm going to take the skirt part off and sew it to this leather T-shirt I bought in the sale in Zara.'

'That sounds really good,' Kitty said. 'That's kind of what we're doing with the film competition at school.'

Dylan nodded. She was leaning forward, her elbows on the table, totally focused on Kitty.

'We're putting old photos of St Margaret's with new stuff we're going to film. We're calling it "The Best of Both Worlds".'

'That sounds brilliant,' Dylan said. 'Seriously!'

Kitty grinned. 'We haven't really done anything yet, though.' She tried to think of something else to say. 'Are you going to study design, do you think?'

'I don't think I'm good enough,' Dylan said. 'Not yet, anyway. But I saw a documentary about Central St Martins – the art school, you know? – and I thought that would be pretty great. How cool would it be to live in London?'

Kitty pictured herself in London with Dylan. Sharing a flat. Studying photography while Dylan studied design. Getting proper coffee (London-Kitty would drink proper coffee) and sitting outside cool cafés. She really had to try to stop her imagination running away with her – it was embarrassing.

'My brother's at uni in London and he loves it,' Kitty said. 'It's only part-time, though, because he has to work. My parents can't afford to pay for him . . .'

'My mum wouldn't either, but my dad might.' Dylan hooked her hair behind one ear and Kitty noticed she had her ear pierced at the top. There was a gold hoop through it. She wanted to reach out and touch it.

But then her gran came back through with cake.

'Oh! I'll help!' Kitty said, jumping up.

She followed her gran through to the kitchen. She needed to calm down before she did something completely idiotic. She ran her hands under the cold tap and patted her hot face, before carrying the pot of tea, cups and saucers back through on a tray.

'This is amazing, Molly,' Dylan said when they were all sitting at the table again.

'I always think if you're going to do afternoon tea you should do it right,' Molly said. 'So sorry I was late, Kitty. We were trying to decide on a charity to support next year. Much argument.' She rolled her eyes.

'Did you settle on one in the end?' Dylan asked.

'I'm settled on one, but I need to convince the breast cancer crowd.'

'Which one do you want?' Dylan said.

'Multiple sclerosis.' Molly topped up her tea, even though she'd only taken a couple of sips. Kitty knew she was just trying to avoid looking at her and she was grateful. She didn't want to talk about it in front of Dylan. She didn't want to get upset in front of her.

'Why multiple sclerosis?' Dylan said. 'I don't really know much about it.'

Molly shook her head. 'That's precisely why. People don't know much about it. Everyone knows about cancer. Cancer should let someone else have a turn.'

Kitty ate her cake and drank her tea and tried to find something to say. She wanted to make sure Dylan would want to hang out with her again. She wanted to be cool and funny and fun so maybe Dylan would ask for her mobile number and maybe they could meet up after school or something. As if.

'So I'm glad you two finally met,' Molly said. 'I thought you'd get on well. Dylan wants to work in fashion,' she told Kitty.

'We were just talking about that,' Kitty said.

'And Kitty . . . Kitty takes wonderful photographs.'

Kitty shook her head.

'You do!' her gran said. 'I've been on your Facebook.'

Kitty snorted and a cake crumb flew across the table. Everyone ignored it.

'Show her,' her gran said. 'On your phone!'

Kitty was saved from having to do this by a knock at the front door. Her gran got up to answer it, muttering to herself about how she was always interrupted and was never allowed five minutes' peace.

'I'd love to see your photos sometime,' Dylan said, turning her cup around in the saucer.

Kitty blushed. 'Oh. They're no big deal, honestly. I don't even have a special camera or anything.'

'It's not about the camera,' Dylan said. She stretched her arm out across the table towards the magazines and Kitty wondered what she'd do if she just reached over and touched it. She just wanted to put her fingers on the back of Dylan's hand or on her wrist where she could see the blue veins just under the surface of her skin. She shook her head. She was doing it again.

'It's nice that your gran's so proud of you,' Dylan said.

Kitty nodded and sipped her tea while she cleared her mind of the image of touching Dylan.

'I am so sorry, girls!' Kitty's gran poked her head through the living room window. 'I completely forgot I'd asked this man to come and measure for bookshelves. Will you be okay on your own for a bit?'

Kitty and Dylan looked at each other. Kitty forced herself to stay quiet. She didn't want Dylan to feel like she'd been trapped into hanging out with her.

'Yeah, that's cool,' Dylan said, smiling at Kitty.

Kitty felt that warm feeling bubbling up inside

again. It didn't mean anything – she was probably just being nice – but at least she'd said yes.

'Maybe you could go next door and show her your room?' Molly said.

Kitty's face burned. How old did her gran think they were? She'd practically suggested they go and play with Dylan's toys together.

'Do you want to?' Dylan asked Kitty.

Kitty's stomach burst into butterflies. She really did.

'If that's okay with you?' she squeaked.

'Excellent!' Molly said. 'I'll bang on the wall when I'm ready for you.'

9

Dylan's bedroom was plainer and brighter than Kitty would have expected. She'd imagined it to be really cool, with posters and photos of Dylan's friends, and maybe candles or lanterns or at least fairy lights, but it had white walls with no posters, and just a few framed photos on top of one of those square bookshelves from IKEA. Her bed was in the far corner, piled with pillows, and on the opposite side of the room there were two small desks, one with a computer and the other with a sewing machine.

'It's just been decorated,' Dylan said, sitting down on a swivel chair near her computer. 'It was the last room in the house to get done. If your gran had suggested we come up here a few weeks ago, I would have had to say no. It had a pink carpet and a Disney Princesses border.'

Kitty laughed. 'You don't like the Disney Princesses?'

Dylan looked like she was actually giving it some thought. 'I like Belle. And Mulan. Is Mulan a princess?'

Kitty frowned. 'I'm not sure. Actually Belle isn't either. But I love Merida.'

'Oh yeah,' Dylan said. 'Merida's awesome.'

They looked at each other and then Dylan said, 'You can sit down, you know. Since you're staying.' She smiled.

'Oh! Yeah. Sorry.'

Kitty looked at the chair next to Dylan's desk, but Dylan pointed at a chair Kitty hadn't even noticed. It was a sort of bouncy rocking chair in the corner, by the window. Kitty lowered herself into it carefully, worried that it would tip up or she'd fall through it or humiliate herself in some other way. She just couldn't seem to properly relax around Dylan.

'It's my sewing chair,' Dylan said. 'Sorry, I'm not really used to having friends round. My school friends all live over on your side and I haven't really met anyone local yet.' She took her phone out of the pocket of her jeans and put it on her bookcase. 'I'm rubbish at this. Do you want a drink or something?'

Kitty shook her head. She didn't know what to do either. She tried to think of what she did when she was round at Sunny's or Hannah's houses, but her mind was pretty much blank. They must do something, of course they did something, but what was it? She had to think, not sit there like a lemon.

'Oh!' Dylan said, so suddenly that Kitty jumped and then blushed. She shifted forward on the chair, but felt it start to tip, so dropped back again.

'You know what you were saying about old photos? I've got a project thing to do for school. Could you help me with it, do you think? We're doing a social history of the town and we're supposed to identify places from old photos using Google Maps and I'm rubbish at it.'

'Yeah, that sounds interesting . . .' Kitty said. But then she worried it had sounded sarcastic. 'I mean it,' she added. 'I mean . . . I'm not being sarcastic.' Oh yes, that was so much better. She wanted to slap herself.

Dylan laughed. 'No, I know you didn't come round to help me with my homework. But it would really help me out.'

'No, really,' Kitty said, finally managing to stand up. 'I want to help.'

Dylan turned on her computer and then went downstairs to get another chair for Kitty to sit on.

While she was waiting for Dylan to come back, Kitty looked through her bookshelves. She had loads of books Kitty had never even heard of, but a few she knew like *Percy Jackson*, *Harry Potter* and *Twilight*.

'Oh god, *Twilight*, I know,' Dylan said, coming back in. 'I loved it, I'm sorry.'

Kitty laughed. 'I loved the first one too. Not the second one, though. And I didn't read the others.'

'I read them all,' Dylan said, her eyes wide. 'And actually I'm not even sorry.'

Kitty laughed.

'Apart from the last one,' Dylan said. 'I am a bit sorry about the last one.'

She'd brought a folding chair with her and she opened it up next to her desk chair.

'So were you Team Edward or Jacob?' Dylan asked, as she fiddled with her computer.

Kitty thought about saying 'Team Bella' but she just couldn't do it.

'A vampire or a werewolf?' she said instead. 'No, thanks.'

Dylan threw a smile back at her. 'I know, right? I'm Team Maybe You're Too Insecure For a Relationship Bella.'

Kitty laughed, but before she had a chance to

respond, Dylan straightened up, and said, 'Okay, this is ready to go.'

Kitty sat down at the computer and, as soon as Dylan sat next to her, she felt like she was too close. But she didn't want to move. She could smell Dylan's shampoo – sort of minty. Or maybe she'd cleaned her teeth when she went to get the chair. But why would she have done that? Unless it was because she knew they'd be sitting close together. Kitty started worrying about her own breath. She tried to push her chair back a bit, but it didn't move. She had to settle for leaning her chin on her hand and putting her fingers over her mouth.

Dylan opened a file full of photographs and clicked on one. It was of a crossroads with a column in the middle. Judging by the cars, Kitty guessed it was maybe the 1940s.

'So this could be anywhere?' Kitty said, frowning.

'No, they're all within this area.' Dylan pointed to the screen. 'I just can't work out which bit's which.'

'So we need to see if we can find that column,' Kitty said. She reached over to the mouse and scrolled around the screen, zooming in and out, swinging the viewpoint around, clicking back to the tiny map for reference.

'There!' she said. She actually felt a tingling run down her arms.

'Wow!' Dylan said. 'That's it! You're really good at this.'

'I like it.' Kitty shrugged. 'I like photos and I like history. And I spend a lot of time on Google Maps.'

Dylan smiled. 'Doing what?'

'Just wandering around . . . Is that sad?'

'No,' Dylan said. 'Show me.' Dylan scooted her chair – hers was on wheels – back a bit and Kitty managed to drag hers forward.

She thought for a second, then typed in 'San Francisco'. The map appeared on the screen and Kitty was just about to zoom closer when Dylan pointed and said, 'Nob Hill? We've got to go there, obviously.'

Kitty laughed. That's exactly what Hannah would have said. She grabbed the little yellow person and dragged and dropped it right next to 'Nob Hill'. The screen filled with a photo of a San Francisco hill – beautiful buildings on each side, cars parked sideways to the kerb and two women with wheelie suitcases crossing the road.

'Which way?' Kitty said.

She swung the compass around and headed up the hill, but that looked like it was mostly hotels. She turned right and right again and then turned the picture full circle.

'Can we go to the beach?' Dylan said, touching the screen where the map showed blue.

Picturing herself and Dylan on the beach together, Kitty zoomed down the main road. But when they got to the ocean, there wasn't a beach and there wasn't a through road. Kitty clicked around a bit and then Dylan said, 'What about the Golden Gate Bridge? Does it let you go across the bridge?'

'I don't know,' Kitty admitted.

She zoomed out and scrolled until she saw what looked like it might be the bridge, but it was really long.

'That must be it, right?'

'Well it goes to Golden Gate National Recreation Area, so I think so . . .' Dylan said.

Kitty dragged the little yellow person to the middle of the bridge and as soon as the picture appeared, she and Dylan both gasped. They were right in the middle of the Golden Gate Bridge, the sun shining on the water, huge American cars in both directions.

'I'd love to go there,' Kitty said. She swung the view around so quickly it made her feel a bit dizzy.

'Me too,' Dylan said. 'Have you ever been to America?'

Dylan shifted in her seat to look at Kitty. Her forearm brushed against Kitty's and Kitty felt goosebumps rise on her skin. She knew Dylan had asked her something, but she couldn't remember what.

She shook her head.

'We went to New York just before my mum and dad split up,' Dylan said. 'I'd love to go back.'

Dylan leaned back in her chair, her arm still resting against Kitty's. Kitty didn't know what to do. Should she move her arm away? She didn't want to. She wanted to move closer. She wanted to run her fingers down Dylan's arm. She wanted to touch her skin. She could see the blonde hairs on Dylan's forearm in the light from the computer screen. She sneaked a look at Dylan, only to see that Dylan was looking straight back at her. She didn't look freaked out. She looked like she was waiting for Kitty to do something.

Kitty jumped as they heard three knocks on the wall.

'My gran,' Kitty said. Her voice came out sounding slightly hysterical.

She didn't want to go, she realised. Even though she was terrified. Even though she had no idea if Dylan was thinking the same things she was thinking, she thought she was – she *hoped* she was – but how could she be sure?

'I'd better go . . .' she said.

She wanted Dylan to say no. To say they should pretend they hadn't heard the knocking. To click return on the search and to spend the rest of the afternoon wandering round America together, if only virtually.

She stood up.

'Wait a sec,' Dylan said.

Kitty's breath caught in her chest.

'Give me your mobile number . . .' Dylan said, fiddling with her own phone.

They swapped numbers and then walked downstairs.

'Are you coming back?' Kitty asked.

Dylan shook her head. 'Better get on with that homework. Now that you've got me off to a good start. Thank you, again. You're brilliant.'

Kitty grinned at her. Dylan thought she was brilliant. She wanted to say 'You're brilliant too' but that would be random, so she didn't.

'Okay then,' she said, instead. 'Bye.'

She practically ran down the path and only looked back when she was through the gate. Dylan waved and Kitty, for some reason, gave her a thumbs up. And then wanted to ram her thumb in her throat. She never did thumbs up! What was she thinking?

Her gran was back in Trevor with a fresh pot of tea and some sort of mesh cover over the cake.

Kitty dropped into her seat. She felt exhausted. Like she'd been trying so hard to hold everything together while she was with Dylan and now she was coming apart.

'She's lovely, isn't she?' her gran said.

Kitty could only nod.

'She had a very sweet friend for a while too . . . She was Elaine's granddaughter. Well, I mean, she still is. She's called Matilda, I think. Or Martha. Something old-fashioned anyway. You remember Elaine? She used to have the tea shop in the park.'

Kitty nodded. She was holding her breath.

'I don't know what happened. They were very sweet together – Dylan and . . . is it Maisie? – and then suddenly . . . she stopped coming round. But that does happen, doesn't it? When you're young?'

Kitty didn't know what to say. She wasn't exactly sure what her gran was trying to tell her. So she just nodded while her gran sipped from her tea, looking at Kitty over the edge of the cup.

All the way home on the train, Kitty went over the conversation with her gran. Did she know? How could she know? Had she been trying to push her and Dylan together?

Or maybe her gran had been saying it was just a phase. She'd said that stuff about Dylan and her 'friend', but she didn't say Maisie – or whatever her name was – was actually Dylan's girlfriend. Maybe she was trying to say, 'You may think you like Dylan, but you're young and you don't really know.'

But Kitty knew that she liked Dylan. She definitely liked Dylan. She rested her head on the window, closed her eyes and pictured herself back in Dylan's room. Sitting close to her on the folding chair. What if she'd just leaned over and kissed her? What would Dylan have done?

Kitty started chewing on her thumbnail. There was no way she could've just kissed Dylan like that. But what if Dylan had kissed her? The thought made her want to leap out of her seat. It was too much to imagine. She went back to thinking about her gran. She hadn't even asked her about the film project, she realised.

As the train came out of the tunnel, Kitty looked out across the estuary as it narrowed into the river. Dylan was over there, behind the wind turbines and the cranes lining the docks. Kitty pictured the Golden

Gate Bridge on Google Maps and imagined herself and Dylan standing there for real, turning round and round. There was no bridge across this river, but there was the train and the ferry and it wasn't so far. She got her phone out and scrolled through to Dylan's name. How mad that she was in her phone. She could ring her if she wanted to. Dylan.

She tapped on the name. She wasn't going to text her; she just wanted to pretend she was going to text her. Her stomach fluttered as she tapped 'text' and stared at the empty box. Then her phone vibrated and pinged and she was so surprised she almost dropped it. A message appeared right there:

Had fun today. Ta for project help. See u soon. Dylan x

Happiness bubbled up through Kitty's chest and she almost laughed out loud. She'd been sitting there staring at Dylan's name and Dylan had been sitting at home – on her bed? At the computer? On the weird bouncy chair? – and looking at Kitty's name. And thinking about texting her. And then Dylan had been brave enough to do it.

Kitty took a deep breath, typed, *I had fun too. Thanx. Kitty xx* and sent it before she could chicken out.

10

Of the three of them, Sunny had the smallest and probably plainest bedroom, but Kitty liked it. It was cosy and den-like and there was a lilac tree right outside her window, which, in the summer, made her room feel a bit like a tree house. Apart from the desk chair and the bed, there was nowhere to sit, so Kitty and Hannah flopped down on the mattress and leaned against the wall, while Sunny turned on her computer.

Her desktop wallpaper was a collage of boys from bands, films and TV – she wasn't allowed posters on her walls so she saved them on her computer instead.

'I read about this website where there's an archive of old photos,' Sunny said, clicking and typing. 'They're free to use.'

Kitty watched her, but all she could think about was the last time she was sitting at a computer, looking at photographs. About what might have happened if she'd put her hand on Dylan's arm. Or moved her chair closer. Or leaned back against her. She'd thought about it so much since the weekend, but she still couldn't imagine herself being able to do it. What if she had, and Dylan had yanked her arm away or said, 'What are you doing?' She'd be mortified. It wasn't worth it. Was it?

She thought about telling Hannah and Sunny. Thought about saying, 'Hey, I've met someone. I really like her. But I don't know what to do.' And then she thought about Mackenzie saying, 'Your lesbo friend' and she knew she couldn't do it. She'd never heard Hannah or Sunny say anything like that, but it wasn't just about them. It was about everyone else. She knew a lot of people at school were more like Mackenzie, people who used 'gay' to mean 'crap' and didn't even think about it. She wasn't ready to deal with it. Not yet. She didn't even know for sure that Dylan was gay.

'This is a good one,' Sunny said, as an old photo of the pier filled the screen.

Kitty and Hannah shuffled across the bed for a closer look. The photo showed the pier absolutely crammed with people. The men were in suits and hats, the women in dresses and high heels. Sunny created a new folder, called it 'film' and dragged the pier photo into it.

'So where else?' she asked.

'How about Vicky Road?' Hannah said. 'I think that used to be pretty cool.'

'Sam was talking about it today,' Kitty said. 'Vicky Road, I mean. Some new café's opened there and there's a taxidermy studio above it.'

'Eww!' Sunny said, swinging round from the computer. 'In a café?!'

'I'm pretty sure he said it's separate,' Kitty said. 'The café's like an American diner, I think, and then upstairs is a shop selling all the stuffed things. And they do classes too.'

'Why was he telling you all this?' Hannah said, grinning at Kitty. 'Does he want you to go on a hot mouse-stuffing date?'

'Eww!' Sunny said again. 'I don't understand why anyone would want to do that. And they look so weird.'

'Not the point, Sun,' Hannah said. 'Sam's trying to tempt Kitty out for burgers followed by . . .' She pulled a rabbity face and held her hands up like claws.

'He wasn't asking me out!' Kitty said, laughing. 'He wasn't even really talking to me. He was just talking.'

'Right,' Hannah said. 'I'm sure. You just can't tell when someone likes you.'

Kitty thought of Dylan and willed herself not to blush. Dylan did like her, didn't she? She wouldn't have texted her if she didn't like her, would she?

'Look at you,' Hannah said, pretending to be proud. 'All moony and in lurve.'

Kitty shoved her and she shrieked, knocking over the can of Coke she'd brought with her. Once they'd cleaned it up, Sunny insisted they get on with looking for more photos. They'd just found a perfect picture of the bandstand with deckchairs lined up in front and people watching a brass band from the hill, when Kitty checked the time on her phone and said, 'Gah. I need to go.'

'I think we've got enough anyway,' Sunny said, swinging round on her chair. 'And I'm starving.'

Kitty and Hannah followed Sunny down the stairs where the smell of spices and coconut wafted out from the kitchen.

'Is that your mum cooking?' Hannah said.

'No, it'll be Dad,' Sunny said, smiling at Hannah and Kitty over her shoulder. 'Mum's taken Hamzah to Mosque for Quran study and then they're picking Aisha up at the food bank. Come and say hello to Dad. He was saying the other day he hasn't seen you for ages.'

'They're still doing the food bank?' Kitty asked. 'How's it going?'

'Aisha loves it,' Sunny said, as they followed her down the hall, the walls covered with family portraits. 'Well, I mean, she doesn't love it, some of it's awful, but she's really into it. I'm going to start going too. In the holidays, when I've got more time.'

'Not if we win the contest,' Kitty said. 'We'll be going on the film-making course.'

'Ooh yeah!' Sunny said. 'London, baby!'

She pushed open the door to the large, bright, kitchen and the three of them burst out laughing at the sight of Sunny's dad.

He was wearing an apron and chef's hat and singing into a wooden spoon.

'Oh Dad!' Sunny said. 'So embarrassing.'

He crossed the room and twirled his daughter. 'Singing is essential while cooking. The beauty of my voice infuses my meals.'

'But your voice is terrible,' Sunny said, grinning. 'It curdles milk.'

'Ah, but it will be beautifully curdled milk.' He nodded at Kitty and Hannah. 'Ladies.'

They both grinned. They loved Sunny's dad.

'Would you two like to stay for dinner?' he asked. 'I've made more than enough.'

Sunny was lifting the lids of pans, sniffing and

stirring. 'He really has,' she said. 'He could feed the whole street.'

'And well I might,' he said. 'Food is best shared.'

'I can't stay,' Kitty said. 'But thank you for asking.'

'No? Got a hot date?'

Kitty flushed as Sunny and Hannah laughed. 'No, no. Got to get home to help my dad make dinner.'

'Your dad's making dinner too?' he said. 'Feminism, eh?' He rolled his eyes, grinning.

'No, Dad,' Sunny said. 'Kitty's mum's ill. You know. I've told you.'

His face turned serious, his eyebrows making a deep V, and Kitty wished Sunny hadn't said anything. She hated the sympathetic looks she got when people talked about her mum.

'How is she?' he asked.

'She's not too bad, thank you,' Kitty said, even though her mum wasn't too good either. 'She's been at the doctors today, actually.'

'You could take some food home?' he suggested. 'Do your parents like Asian food?'

Kitty nodded. 'They do. But Dad will have already started on tonight's. Thank you, though.'

Sunny's dad gave a sort of bow and then turned to Hannah. 'You will stay!'

Hannah nodded. 'Yes, please.'

He pinched her cheek. 'Good. You need fattening up.'

'Dad!' Sunny shrieked. 'Oh my god!'

Kitty's stomach rumbled as she walked home through the park. She would have loved to have stayed at Sunny's for dinner. She would have loved to have taken some food home. Actually, maybe she should have said yes anyway. Whatever her dad was making was probably a bit dull and tasteless in comparison. They used to sometimes get an Indian takeaway on the Friday after Dad had been paid and Kitty loved how they all shared the food – everyone had a bit of everything. Poppadoms snapping and food getting spilled and staining the tablecloth. Her dad letting her taste his Cobra beer and her mum pretending to disapprove. She couldn't remember the last time they'd done that. But meals at Sunny's house were like that all the time.

She hated envying her friends. She'd always felt lucky in the past. Lucky to have parents who loved her and loved each other. Lucky to have Tom and Grace and lucky to live where she lived. But she didn't feel so lucky any more. And she hated feeling that way.

11

'How did you get on?' Kitty asked her dad when she got home. He was putting the shopping away, and had bags all over the kitchen floor.

'With what?' he asked, stuffing a huge bag of frozen peas into the freezer. 'I got those crinkle-cut chips you like.'

'At the doctor's,' Kitty said. 'I saw it on the calendar.' She pulled an out-of-date school timetable off the side of the fridge and dropped it in the recycling bin.

'Oh.' Her dad closed the fridge door and leaned back against it, looking at Kitty. 'Honestly, Kit, you don't need to worry about it,'

'But I am worried,' Kitty said. 'What did the doctor say?'

'Honestly, it's nothing. Your mum's just been feeling a bit . . . low.' He bent down and picked up a four-pack of baked beans and put them in the cupboard. 'She wanted to get some advice about that. But she doesn't want you worrying about it.'

'I'll worry more if you don't tell me things!' Kitty realised her voice was slightly too loud, but she was sick of her dad telling her she didn't need to worry. How did he not get that it only made her worry more?

He closed the cupboard, and looked at Kitty again. 'Okay. You're right. Sorry. She's given her some tablets.'

'What for?' Kitty frowned.

'To make her feel a bit more cheerful. And she's put her forward for a trial. You know, a clinical trial thing?'

Kitty nodded. She'd read about that online. There were lots of different trials all the time. And just because her mum had been put forward for one didn't mean she was going to get on it.

'What kind of a trial?'

'Not really sure of the details yet, but it sounded interesting. And even if she doesn't get on this one, they can put her name down for the next one. It made your mum feel much brighter,' he said. 'It's been hard for her feeling like there's nothing she can do.'

Kitty nodded. She'd felt helpless since the day she first found out, so she could imagine how much worse it must be for her mum.

'Do you want to take her a tea up?' her dad said, getting two mugs out of the cupboard.

'Yeah,' Kitty said. 'In a minute.' She leaned back against the radiator, which was freezing cold against the backs of her legs. 'Grace asked me some stuff the other day. She was a bit upset.'

Her dad filled the kettle, then turned to look at Kitty. Kitty could see how tired he was – he had blue smudges under his eyes and he hadn't shaved – and she felt suddenly guilty for saying anything at all. But it wasn't fair that she had to answer Grace's questions. She didn't want to get anything wrong.

'What did she want to know?' her dad asked.

'She was worried that maybe it's hereditary,' Kitty said. 'I told her that it's not, but ...'

Her dad shook his head.

'And she was asking if Mum's going to ...' Kitty had prepared what she was going to say in her head before she opened her mouth, but now she was saying it she found she couldn't. She couldn't say 'die'. She could hear it in her head, but ...

Her dad crossed the kitchen in a couple of strides and pulled Kitty against him, squeezing her so hard she almost wanted him to stop.

'I'm so sorry,' he said. 'I've done a terrible job of

talking to you two about this.'

'Not terrible,' Kitty squeaked, her face pressed up against his chest. She could smell his lemony aftershave and the fabric softener from his jumper.

'Not good,' he said. She felt him kiss the top of her head. 'I'll talk to your sister,' he said.

Kitty squeezed him back.

'And you're okay, are you?' he said into her hair.

Kitty nodded. 'I've read some stuff. It's scary, but I'm okay.'

Her mum definitely did look better, Kitty thought. She was sitting up against the pillows, reading. She had her glasses on and, when she saw Kitty, she smiled. It wasn't her old smile – that was almost dazzling and always made Kitty smile back without even thinking about it. This was a sadder smile.

The room seemed a bit brighter too – the curtains weren't fully closed and the window was open so it was fresher. Kitty felt like she could breathe.

'How you doin', kid?' her mum said in an American accent.

Kitty smiled. 'I'm okay.'

'How was school?'

Kitty sat down on the bed and told her mum about

the photos they'd found at Sunny's. 'So now we need to go and film all the same places, looking busy and more fun.'

'Sounds like it's going to be good, this film,' her mum said.

Kitty nodded. 'I think so. Sunny's determined we're going to win. She's already making lists of what we're going to do in London.'

'It would be lovely for you to go,' her mum said. She reached up and pushed Kitty's fringe out of her eyes. 'Nice to see Tom.'

Kitty nodded.

'Do you miss him?'

Kitty nodded again.

'Me too. Stay with me for a bit?' her mum asked.

She hadn't said that for ages. When she was first ill, Kitty used to stay in the room with her and do her homework while her mum read, but after a while her mum was sleeping more than reading and it was easier for Kitty to get her homework done on the dining table or in her own room.

She kicked off her shoes and crawled up the bed to sit next to her mum, her dad's pillow behind her. She looked across at the family photos on the opposite wall. This felt like how things used to be. Before her mum started having numb fingers and dropping things and feeling weird sensations in her legs. Before the doctors thought it was a slipped disc or a trapped nerve or even stress. Before multiple sclerosis changed everything.

'Kitty . . .'

Kitty looked down and traced her finger along one of the navy stripes on the duvet cover. She knew her mum's 'serious' voice instantly.

'Listen to me, please.'

Kitty looked up. Her mum had that little frown line between her eyebrows.

'I'm sorry I haven't been around,' she said. 'This hit me . . . harder than I would have expected. As wonderful as your dad is, I know you need me too. I'm going to try harder to be around more. Did your dad tell you we've been to the doctor today?'

Kitty nodded.

'She was great and we got some medication. It'll take a couple of weeks to take effect, but it really should help. So no more lying around in bed. I'm not promising things will go back to normal – or anything like it really – but . . .'

Her voice had started to crack and she put her hand up to her mouth.

Kitty looked at the photos again. The biggest one was of the five of them – her parents, herself, Grace and Tom – sitting on a wall on the prom, all squinting into the sun. Grace was wearing wellies, even though it was summer. They were Hello Kitty and she wore them for about a year when she was five. She never wanted to take them off.

'I'm so proud of you,' her mum said. 'I hope you know that. And I hope you know that if you need to talk to me about anything at all, I'm always here. Literally.' She bumped Kitty with her shoulder to make her laugh.

Kitty smiled, but her eyes filled with tears. First her dad and now her mum. She nodded, but she couldn't speak.

12

Kitty sat down at her desk to do her homework, but she couldn't concentrate. She'd always talked to her mum about everything and, even though her mum said she still could, she just didn't feel the same. She knew neither her mum nor her dad really wanted to talk about the MS. They mentioned it as little as possible and in very vague detail and they both still got upset about it easily. And Kitty definitely couldn't talk to her mum about Dylan, even though she wanted to.

She rested her head on her arms on the desk and closed her eyes. And then almost immediately sat straight up. Did her mum already know about Dylan? Had her gran talked to her? It seemed strange that she'd suddenly said Kitty could talk to her about anything. Was that a hint? Was she trying to make it easier for her to tell her?

Kitty tried to imagine telling her mum about Dylan, but she couldn't. She tried to think what she'd say if

Dylan was a boy. 'I've met a boy and I really like him' somehow seemed much easier than 'I've met a girl and I really like her'. Even though she knew her parents had been fine when Tom had come out to them.

He'd been older than Kitty, but not much, and he'd told Mum and Dad one night when they were watching TV, after Kitty had gone to bed. He told her later that he'd been planning it for ages, but kept freaking out and putting it off until he just forced himself to say it. He said it was brilliant because they'd had a quick chat and a hug and then all gone back to watching *Have I Got News For You*. From then on they all talked about it openly and now Kitty felt like she'd always known.

She clicked her mouse to wake her computer up. She needed to talk to Tom.

He answered almost immediately, but to begin with there was no picture. They had the usual five minutes of clicking on stuff and hearing Tom saying, 'Can you see me now?' and then finally his face appeared – grinning, as usual.

Kitty was shocked at how happy she was to see him. She hadn't realised she'd been so tensed up until she felt herself relax.

'What are you doing?' Kitty said.

'I was working on an essay,' Tom said. 'So I'm

very happy to stop and talk to my little sis. Where's my littlest sis?'

'Downstairs. Helping Dad make tea.'

'Egg and chips?' Tom said and smiled.

'Probably.' Kitty smiled back. It was good to see his face.

'How's Mum?' her brother asked.

'Slightly better. We had a bit of a talk earlier. I think the doctor's put her on antidepressants.'

Tom's eyes went wide. 'How come?'

Kitty shook her head. She didn't want to worry him too much because there was nothing he could do from London.

'I think she was just finding it all . . . hard to deal with. But it's going to get better now, I'm sure.'

'Is Dad doing okay? I know he's having to work more.'

'Yeah. He's his usual self, you know? Pretends everything's fine most of the time.'

'He told me everything's fine.'

'Yeah. I mean . . . it hasn't been. But I think it's going to be.'

Tom frowned and swigged from a bottle of water. 'You know you can always talk to me, Kit. If you're worried.'

Kitty nodded. 'That's sort of why I Skyped.'

'Uh-oh,' Tom said. 'Are you okay?'

'I'm fine. I . . . I sort of . . . like someone.'

Tom beamed at her and she found herself grinning back.

'Who is he? Tell me everything.'

'He is, um . . . a she.' Kitty blew out her breath and leaned forward to concentrate on her brother's face.

'Whoa!' said Tom, his eyebrows shooting up. 'Really?'

Kitty nodded. She couldn't tell what he thought.

Tom pulled a bewildered face. 'But you can't be gay, Kits. I'm gay.'

Kitty barked with laughter. 'You didn't bagsy gay, Tom. I'm allowed to be gay too.'

'God, you always were a copycat.'

Kitty sat back in her chair and wrinkled her nose. 'I've been worrying about that a bit . . .'

'What? That you copied gay off me?' Tom laughed again. 'I don't think it works like that.'

'I know it doesn't really. I just . . . Isn't it weird that we'd both be gay?'

Tom shook his head. 'I don't think so. It's not catching – I don't know anyone who's gay because their brother or sister was first. It's just one of those things. Seriously.' He smiled. 'So tell me about the girl.'

Kitty's stomach fluttered. 'She's . . . amazing.'

'Name?'

'Dylan.'

'Dylan? You're sure she's a girl, not a girly boy?'

Kitty laughed. 'No, she's a girl.'

'And you like her?'

'I do, yeah.'

'Have you told Mum and Dad?'

'I haven't told anyone. It's pretty much all I think about, but I can't make it come out of my mouth. I'm doing my own head in.'

'Have you gone out? You and Dylan?'

Kitty shook her head. 'No. That's the other thing. I don't even know if she likes me. I don't even know for sure that she's gay. Gran was hinting about it, but –'

Tom sat up so fast, the top of his head disappeared off the screen. 'Gran?! Have you talked to her? About this?'

'No. But I think she knows. Or suspects. About me, I mean. Do you think she could?'

Tom leaned forward, his chin on his hand. 'Probably. She doesn't miss much.'

'She knows Dylan. Dylan lives next door to her. She loves Gran.'

'I like the sound of her already. So you don't know for sure that Dylan's gay and Dylan doesn't know you like her?'

Kitty shook her head. 'I don't think so, no. Maybe. I mean, I act like an idiot around her, so maybe she does? Or maybe she just thinks I'm an idiot.'

'Not possible. So. You know what I'm going to say, don't you?'

'No.' She really didn't.

'You need to ask her out.'

Kitty shook her head. 'Oh god.'

'You do, Kits. You like her and you need to know if she likes you. There's only one way to find out.'

'Can you do it for me? I'll give you her mobile . . .'

Tom laughed. 'Yeah. No. Do it right now, before you chicken out.'

'I never chickened in.'

'Do it,' Tom said. 'And then Skype me and tell me how it went.'

After she'd logged off from Skype, Kitty made herself do exactly what Tom said. Straight away, before she got scared and changed her mind. She scrolled to Dylan's profile in her phone and touched 'call mobile'. Her hands were shaking and she felt like she might throw up, but she pressed the phone to her ear and took deep breaths until she heard Dylan answer.

'Hi,' Kitty said. 'It's Kitty.'

'I know,' Dylan said. 'You're in my phone. I was just thinking about you.'

Kitty's stomach flipped over painfully. 'Were you?'

'Yeah. I got tickets to the River Festival, you know, at the pier? I was wondering if maybe you wanted to come?'

Kitty's breathing felt ragged. 'Yes,' she said. 'That would be fab.'

'It's this Saturday,' Dylan said. 'Short notice, sorry.'

'Oh! Yeah, sorry, didn't even think . . . Yeah, that's fine. I'm sure. I don't have any plans or anything.'

'Great,' Dylan said. 'So . . . what were you phoning for?'

Kitty's mind went completely blank. 'I was just going to see if . . .' She looked around the room as if some sort of answer would present itself. But she obviously couldn't say she'd phoned to talk about her wardrobe. Or the PE bag at the foot of her bed.

'I just wanted to ask if you wanted to hang out maybe,' she said eventually.

'After school?' Dylan said.

'Um. No. I've got the film to do, you know? I

meant at the weekend or whenever, but then you said about the festival, so . . .'

'Great minds,' Dylan said.

'Yeah,' Kitty said. 'So, um, Saturday then?'

'Yeah. It starts at one, so do you want to meet at half twelve? You'll be getting the ferry?'

'Yes.'

'Okay. I'll meet you off the ferry then and we can walk over,' Dylan said.

'Great,' Kitty said. She wanted to say she couldn't wait. That she was really looking forward to it. But she didn't dare. Also, it wasn't strictly true, because she was as scared as she was excited.

'See you Saturday then.'

'Yes,' Kitty said.

She pressed 'end call' and then hit herself on the forehead with the phone.

13

The first time Kitty got the ferry she was a toddler. Her parents thought she'd love it, but she'd been terrified and had spent the whole journey inside, sitting under a table with her hands over her ears. Tom had laughed at her so much that Dad had taken him outside and a seagull had swooped down and knocked his crisps out of his hand, so he'd ended up howling too. It was one of their dad's favourite stories.

The next time she got it she was with Hannah. They were eleven and neither of them was allowed to get the ferry on their own, but Hannah decided this meant they could go together and even though Kitty knew that wasn't right, she went all the same. Sunny was on holiday, but she wouldn't have gone with them anyway. And she would have talked Kitty out of it too. Hannah and Kitty had stood up on the railings trying to get the spray in their hair until a guard had shouted at them to get down.

This time, Kitty bought herself a can of Coke and sat outside, at the front, on one of the slatted wooden seats, so she could watch the town – and the pier – coming closer. She felt almost sick with nerves, but decided the best way to deal with it was to face it. Otherwise she was worried she'd hide inside until the ferry turned round and returned her to St Margaret's.

She'd actually lost sleep trying to decide what to wear and had eventually decided on a red-and-white-striped T-shirt and cut-off jeans with her yellow Converse. Now she wasn't sure if it was all too bright, too Where's Wally, and maybe she should have tried to be cooler. She'd Googled the festival and there was a mix of bands – from pop to indie and even a Queen tribute band, so she really had no idea.

The ferry hooted the horn as they approached the pier and Kitty put both hands on her stomach to calm the churning. What if it wasn't just Dylan? What if it was a group thing and Kitty had to spend the day with a bunch of people she'd never met? What if Dylan had guessed Kitty had a crush on her and the whole thing was a joke and Dylan wasn't even there? What if she *was* there? What if Dylan liked her too and this was a date? That was the scariest scenario of them all. Just the thought made Kitty suck in her breath and press herself back against the wooden seat. She gulped some Coke. Her hands were shaking.

Kitty saw Dylan before Dylan saw her. She was at the top of the ramp, clearly looking for someone, frowning and scanning the crowd. She was wearing cut-off jeans too, and flip-flops with a Cookie Monster T-shirt. Kitty thought about waving, but that felt too embarrassing, so she was actually quite close to Dylan when Dylan finally spotted her.

'Hey!' Dylan grinned at her. 'I was worried you'd missed this one.'

Kitty noticed Dylan had her phone in her hand. Had she really been worried Kitty wouldn't turn up? Like that was ever going to happen.

'You're allowed to take your own food in,' Dylan said, as they walked away from the terminal, 'so I thought we could go up to the Co-op and get some stuff?'

'Okay,' Kitty said.

She looked over at Pier Gardens. She'd seen the stage set up from the ferry, but she hadn't seen how many people were there. The grass was covered with blankets and those little fold-up chairs, and there were people sitting on the walls outside.

'It's really busy!' Kitty said.

'Yeah, well, that boy band is on – you know from *X Factor*? I think they're on first though so loads of these girls will go afterwards, I think.'

Kitty nodded. She wasn't sure which band Dylan meant and didn't like to ask, but she'd find out soon enough. They walked up Lyon Street and Dylan talked about Campbell, a girl singer she liked and the reason she'd wanted to come to the festival in the first place. Kitty hadn't heard of her either.

As they walked, Dylan told her about a man on the bus who'd staggered from the back to the front when the driver had slammed on the brakes and had then complained about it for the rest of the journey. Kitty told her the ferry story about Tom and the seagulls, but her heart wasn't really in it. She was so aware of Dylan alongside her she felt like she was glowing, like she had a force field around herself.

In the Co-op Dylan grabbed a basket and said, 'What do you like? We need drinks – plastic bottles are allowed, I looked it up – and then, I don't know, stuff that's not going to melt?'

Kitty grabbed a bag of popcorn that was on special offer.

'Good call,' Dylan said.

'It's my sister's favourite,' Kitty said. 'There's a Co-op at the top of our road.'

'So you've got skillz,' Dylan said, grinning and reaching for a packet of Haribo.

'Yeah,' Kitty said. 'Food shopping skillz. Useful.'

Dylan seemed to be grabbing things off the shelves without looking at the prices or even thinking about how much food they'd need. She just kept saying, 'This?' and then throwing it in. Kitty had taken twenty pounds out of her savings account, but she really hoped she wouldn't have to spend it all, not least because her parents would go mad when they realised. She'd sneaked the paying-in book out of her Mum's bedroom drawer.

When they got to the counter, Kitty took the twenty-pound note out of the tiny pocket in the front of her jeans, but Dylan waved it away.

'Don't worry, I've got money from my dad. Guilt money.'

Kitty raised her eyebrows.

'He was supposed to be coming this weekend, but he cancelled.'

'Where does he live?'

Dylan paid and Kitty lifted the bag of shopping off the counter.

'Just outside Manchester,' Dylan said. 'He's meant to come every other weekend, but he cancels more than he comes. He's got five kids, sort of, so I know he's got other stuff, but still . . .'

'Sort of?' Kitty said.

She thought about what it would be like to only see her dad every couple of weekends. Yes, he was driving her a bit mad at the minute, but she hated the idea of not seeing him every day.

'Laura – his wife – she already had three,' Dylan said, as they left the shop and the heat hit them. 'And now they've got two more together. Your parents are still together, right?' Dylan said. 'Have you just got the one sister?'

Kitty shook her head. 'No, my brother Tom's at university in London.'

'Oh yeah, sorry.' They stopped at the pedestrian crossing. 'I remember you saying that when we were at your gran's.'

Kitty tried not to be pleased that Dylan had remembered, but she failed. She smiled to herself.

'How old are your dad's children?' she asked, as they crossed the road.

'Charlie's four and Gaby's two. They're really cute. And then Laura's kids are, I don't know, I think

Cameron is ten – he's a bit weird, talks about *Minecraft* all the time – and Jake and Toby are fourteen.'

'Same as me,' Kitty said. She'd been worrying that Dylan maybe thought she was older.

'Are you?' Dylan said, smiling at her. 'I'm fifteen. But only just. Last week.'

'Oh!' Kitty said. 'I wish I'd known!'

'You'd've baked me a cake?' Dylan said, smiling.

Kitty blushed. 'I might've texted you . . . a photo of a cake.'

Dylan grinned. 'When's yours?'

'December,' Kitty said. But they hadn't really celebrated it last year because they'd just found out about her mum's MS.

'So there's, like, six months between us,' Dylan said.

They waited at the lights to cross to Pier Gardens. Kitty looked back across the river, where she'd just come from, and wondered what her friends were doing. There was no way they would ever imagine she was over here at the festival. With a girl. She felt guilty when she thought about not telling them. She'd have to make herself not think about them or she wouldn't be able to relax.

14

Kitty and Dylan crossed the main road to Pier Gardens and negotiated the crowd waiting outside. At the gate Dylan handed the tickets over to a woman in a high-vis jacket. Once security had looked in the Co-op bag, Dylan and Kitty were waved through.

'Where do you want to sit?' Dylan asked.

Kitty looked around. She couldn't see any spaces. It was really crowded. Along the back were food trucks and Kitty could already smell chips, burgers, popcorn and something else – something that smelled like burned chocolate. There were loads of people standing, but also plenty of groups sitting with picnic blankets and even buggies. She couldn't see anywhere to sit.

'Oh wait, look!' Dylan said, pointing past the trucks. Kitty couldn't see what she was pointing at, but she followed her as she picked her way through the crowd.

Every few steps Dylan glanced back to check that

Kitty was still behind her. It made her stomach flutter. She tried to keep up, but when she got caught in one of those 'no, you first' dances with a man and a little boy, she lost sight of Dylan. Once the man was out of the way, she saw her, waiting for Kitty in front of the desk with the tech for filming the performances.

As Dylan watched her approach, Kitty tugged at her T-shirt and tucked her hair back behind her ears.

'Just here,' Dylan said, when Kitty reached her. She stepped over a small wall and sat down on a grassy mound. It was just in front of a statue of some famous musician from the fifties, and she and Kitty were the only people sitting there.

'Wow,' Kitty said. 'This is brilliant.'

Dylan grinned. 'I sat here last year. I don't know why, but there was no one here then either.'

'It's a really good view.'

'I think people feel they need to get closer, but there's a better view from far away. And if it rains we can shelter under the statue.'

Kitty looked up at the clear blue sky. 'I don't think that's going to be a problem today . . .'

She stretched her legs out in front of her and put the Co-op bag between herself and Dylan. Dylan was sitting with one leg tucked underneath her and the other stretched out. She'd kicked off her flip-flops. Her toenails were painted neon yellow.

'Are you hungry?' Dylan asked.

Kitty was still too nervous to be really hungry, but she nodded. She took a bottle of water out of the bag and Dylan opened the popcorn.

The stage lights flashed on and off and Kitty blinked. She hadn't been to a gig for ages. In fact, she'd only ever been to a couple – one with Hannah and one when she was ten with her mum. And that was an Abba tribute so it probably didn't count.

'Help yourself to everything,' Dylan said.

Kitty reached into the popcorn and took out a handful. She could hear Dylan munching. A local radio DJ came on stage and tried to get the crowd to chant the name of the festival's sponsors along with him, but the girls at the front were screaming too loudly for it to work, so he gave up and announced the *X Factor* band.

'They're rubbish,' Dylan said. 'But I do quite like this song.'

Kitty nodded. It was okay. She couldn't hear it very well over the screaming. She reached her hand into the popcorn bag, but touched Dylan's hand rather than popcorn. She pulled her hand out and felt her face get hot. She glanced at Dylan out of the corner of her eye, but she didn't seem to have noticed. She was eating the popcorn and looking over at the stage.

The *X Factor* band did three songs and then the DJ came back on again and started trying to get people up on stage for some competition.

Kitty kept drinking her water and trying not to look at Dylan. But all she wanted to do was look at Dylan. She really liked her face. She had proper cheekbones that looked like she was sucking her cheeks in. And she had really nice eyes – she was obviously good at putting on make-up because her eyeliner had little flicks on the end. Kitty had tried that, but could only do it on her right eye and not her left.

Dylan caught Kitty looking at her and smiled.

'They were better than I thought they were going to be,' Dylan said.

'They were okay,' Kitty agreed.

'Not into boy bands then?' Dylan asked, smiling and unscrewing the top of a bottle of water.

'Not really, no,' Kitty said. 'I don't really listen to a lot of music. I mean ... I don't usually know anything new.'

'You like old stuff? Like what?'

'My mum used to always have the radio on at home, but it was almost always an eighties station.'

Dylan grinned. 'So . . . Wham!?'

Kitty fiddled with the laces of her Converse. 'I like Wham!, yeah. And Duran Duran.'

'I hate to break this to you,' Dylan said, 'but they were boy bands.'

Kitty laughed. 'Yeah, I suppose so. They didn't do dance routines though.'

'Oh yeah, that makes all the difference.' She put the bottle of water down and picked up a carton of raspberries. 'I like some old stuff too. Do you know Blondie?'

'Yes! My mum loves them! And I love that song, "Atomic".' The line in that song about someone's hair being beautiful popped into Kitty's head and she couldn't resist looking over at Dylan again. Her hair *was* beautiful. The sun made it look more red than purple and it was almost glowing.

Dylan looked at her and smiled, and then looked back towards the stage.

'My ex-girlfriend was all about the boy bands,' she said.

Kitty's stomach lurched and her toes curled up inside her shoes.

'I actually queued with her for One Direction tickets,' Dylan said. 'Six hours.'

'Must've been love,' Kitty managed to say, although it came out as a whisper.

Dylan pulled a face. 'Not really, no.'

'Oh,' Kitty said. 'Sorry. I was joking, I didn't mean . . .'

'No, I know,' Dylan said, smiling. 'I only brought it up because . . . I . . .' She looked down at her hands and it was the first time Kitty had seen her look nervous. 'Because I wasn't sure if you knew I was gay. And I wanted to make sure you did. Know, I mean.'

Kitty realised she was biting her thumbnail and pulled her hand out of her mouth. 'I did know,' she said. 'I mean . . . I thought so. My gran said something that made me think . . .'

Dylan laughed. 'Wow, really? I think my nanna's still telling people I'm going through a funny phase.'

Kitty wasn't sure what she was supposed to say to that.

'So . . .' Dylan said. 'How about you? Going through a "funny phase"?'

Kitty frowned. 'I don't think so . . .' She shook her head. That sounded awful. 'I mean, I don't have any experience of anything, so . . .'

'Never had a boyfriend?' Dylan asked.

'Nope. A boy pushed me up against a wall at a party and kissed me. I didn't like it. But I knew him at primary school when he used to wave his thing at everyone in PE, so I probably wouldn't have liked it anyway.'

Dylan threw her head back and laughed. 'I've never even kissed a boy. Or been kissed by one. Even a gross one. I've known since I was about seven, I think . . .'

'Wow,' Kitty said. 'Really? That's . . . amazing. I don't think I'd even thought about it at that age.'

'I had a crush on Alex in *Wizards of Waverly Place*. That was a couple of years later, but that's when my mum started to wonder.'

'Does she know?' Kitty asked, although she suspected she knew the answer.

Dylan nodded. 'She's great. She's always just told me to be whoever I am, you know? My dad knows, but he pretends he doesn't . . . How about you? Have you told anyone?'

'I've talked to my brother – he's gay . . . too. But I wasn't sure there was anything to tell.' She stared at her shoes and then looked back at Dylan. She took a deep breath. 'Until I met you.'

Dylan stared at her. 'Really?'

Kitty nodded. She could feel her heart hammering in her chest. 'I always thought I didn't really need to think about it until I met someone. Or, I mean,

I thought I wouldn't know for sure until I met someone. Whether that was a boy or a girl, you know? But then I saw you and . . .'

'You couldn't stop thinking about me?' Dylan said, smiling at her from under her fringe.

Kitty nodded. She didn't have enough breath to speak.

'I know, cos I was the same. About you, I mean.'

'Really?' Kitty said. 'I thought you probably thought I was the weird girl who couldn't even talk properly around you.'

'Well . . . that too.' Dylan grinned.

Kitty threw a piece of popcorn at her. 'It was hard for me! To talk to you.'

'You're not doing so badly now,' Dylan said.

'No,' Kitty said. Even so, she couldn't quite believe they were even having this conversation.

The DJ announced Campbell, and Dylan stood up and reached down to pull Kitty up with her. And then she just kept hold of her hand.

Campbell was fantastic. Kitty hadn't known her music at all, but she'd loved it. What she'd heard of it. She had spent quite a lot of time focused on Dylan's hand. The feel of her skin, her fingers occasionally squeezing

Kitty's. Just the idea that Dylan was holding her hand. She was holding Dylan's hand. It made her feel like she could really do this, she could really be with Dylan.

But then, after the Queen tribute band had done a few songs, it had clouded over and started to rain. Dylan had mimed that maybe they should go – the Queen band were really loud – and Kitty had to let go of Dylan's hand to pick up what was left of their stuff. She felt a bit lost without it, which was ridiculous since she'd had fourteen years without it and less than an hour with it, but her hand felt cold and weird on its own.

As Dylan stepped over the small wall to make their way back to the gate, she reached out to Kitty and, just as Kitty was about to take her hand, she saw Amber's long blonde hair and *You Wish!* T-shirt. She was only a couple of metres in front of the wall. Had she been there the entire time? Kitty looked around in panic in case Mackenzie was there too, but she couldn't see her. Just Amber. She was rummaging in her bright pink Paul's Boutique bag and then she pulled out an umbrella.

Kitty turned back to Dylan, who'd put her hand down and was staring at her. She looked confused.

'I just . . . I saw someone from school,' Kitty said.

'A friend?'

Kitty shook her head. 'No, really, no.'

'Does it matter if she saw us then?' Dylan said, shrugging.

Kitty's stomach was churning. 'I don't think she did,' she said.

Dylan gave her an odd look, but Kitty couldn't really think about what it meant. All she could think about was whether Amber had seen them.

She followed Dylan back through the crowd to the exit, holding the Co-op bag over her head to keep off the rain.

15

'Where were you on Saturday?' Hannah asked Kitty, as they walked to school. 'James wanted to go bowling and I said I'd only come if you came too, but you didn't answer your phone.'

'Your mum's still seeing him?' Sunny said.

'Yep. They were all over each other this weekend. It was gross.'

The three of them got halfway across the road and waited on the traffic island.

'Kitty?' Hannah said. 'Where were you?'

Kitty stared straight ahead, focusing on the school railings, trying to concentrate on her breathing. 'I went to the River Festival.'

'Oh wow, did you?' Sunny said. 'I wanted to go to that, but I wasn't allowed. Of course. Who did you go with?'

'Um . . .' Kitty said. She took a deep breath. 'Someone I'm sort of seeing.'

'Shut. Up,' Sunny said, excitedly. 'Who? Where did you meet him? What's he like? What did you do?'

Kitty felt like she was going to be sick. She tried to say 'It's not a boy, it's a girl', but she just couldn't make it come out of her mouth.

'Come on!' Hannah said, as they crossed the rest of the road. 'Tell us everything. Who is he? Where did you meet him? Why have you been keeping him secret?'

As they walked through the school gates, Kitty said it again in her head – 'It's not a boy, it's a girl' – but then she thought about the follow-up questions: 'How long have you known you were gay?' 'Have you liked any other girls?' and she just couldn't do it.

'He lives next door to my gran,' she said.

'Ooh!' Hannah said, grinning. 'Literally the boy next door! Nice.'

'So how come you ended up going to the festival with him?' Sunny said, dodging a boy on a bike.

'He rang and asked me,' Kitty said. 'I think he had a spare ticket . . . someone cancelled or something.'

'Oh that's such a cliché,' Hannah said. 'He bought the tickets so then he could say "Uh, I've got tickets for this thing . . . no big deal." I bet he's been eyeing you up for ages.'

Kitty shook her head. 'He's not lived there long.'

'So was it good? Are you seeing him again?'

'Seeing who again?' the boy on the bike said, pulling up alongside them.

'Seriously, Sam,' Sunny said. 'You're going to get a reputation as a stalker.'

'And it's none of your business anyway,' Hannah said.

'All right,' Sam said. 'Keep your hair on. I was only asking!'

Kitty was glad of the distraction. Why had she even told them? Why hadn't she made up some story about where she was and why she missed Hannah's call? Stupid.

'So are you?' Hannah asked, as Sam cycled away, his hands ostentatiously behind his head. 'Seeing him again?'

'I'm not sure,' Kitty said. 'We didn't make any plans or anything.'

'What's his name?' Hannah asked.

'Dylan,' Kitty said. At least she could tell the truth about that.

'Did you kiss?' Sunny asked.

'They did,' Hannah said, turning to peer directly at Kitty's face. 'Look, she's gone bright red.'

Kitty put her hands up to her face. 'I don't want to talk about this!'

Hannah and Sunny roared with laughter.

'We'll get it out of you,' Hannah said. 'You can't keep secrets from us!'

That was what Kitty was afraid of.

'Have you got my notebook?' Sunny asked Kitty as they walked up to Ms Guyomar's room at lunchtime. The teacher had left a note in each of their lockers asking them to come for a preliminary meeting to discuss their plans for the film.

'I don't think so,' Kitty said. She opened her bag and rummaged through her books. 'No, sorry.'

'Bum,' Sunny said. 'Can't find it.'

'Which notebook?'

'The one for the film. I know we haven't started filming yet, but I thought we could show her our plans, at least.'

'Maybe Hannah's got it,' Kitty said.

'Maybe,' Sunny agreed.

Hannah was already there when Kitty and Sunny arrived. And so was Louis. They were sitting on separate desks, but they were talking. Hannah was laughing and Louis was grinning back at her.

'Whoa,' Kitty heard Sunny whisper.

She'd been thinking the same thing. If it had been Mackenzie and Amber who'd walked in and seen that, Hannah would be dead meat.

'Have you got my notebook?' Sunny asked Hannah.

Hannah looked startled. And Kitty thought she was even blushing a bit. That wasn't good at all. Why was she even talking to him after what she'd told them in the park? Unless she was still trying to wind Mackenzie up. But why did she even care?

Hannah shook her head. 'Haven't seen it, sorry.'

Kitty and Sunny sat down, then Mrs Guyomar came in, followed by Mackenzie and Amber, who acted like Kitty, Hannah and Sunny weren't even there. Kitty sneaked looks at Amber, trying to work out if she'd seen her with Dylan, but Amber just chatted to Mackenzie and didn't even look at her.

'So do you want to show me what you've got so far?' the teacher said.

'We haven't actually done much filming yet,' Kitty said.

'We have!' Mackenzie said. 'Do you want to see?'

She pushed their camera – which was definitely more impressive-looking than the one Ms Guyomar

124

had given them – across her desk and sat back with a smug grin on her face.

'What's the idea?' Ms Guyomar said, flipping out the screen and pressing play.

'We've got old photos and then we've filmed the same places now, to show how it's good for young people and old people,' Mackenzie said.

Kitty looked over at Sunny, who was looking stunned and shaking her head.

'Are you JOKING?!' Sunny said.

'What's wrong?' Ms Guyomar asked, looking at Sunny over the top of her glasses.

'That's our idea,' Kitty said.

Ms Guyomar laughed. 'Oh dear. Well, it's a good idea . . .'

'No,' Sunny said. 'They stole it.'

Mackenzie, Amber and Louis all laughed.

'As if!' Mackenzie said, her pencil-thin eyebrows shooting up near her hairline.

'So it's just a coincidence that I can't find my notebook that would show it was our idea and you've done the same thing as us?' Sunny said.

'I'm sure it is,' Ms Guyomar said. 'This happens more than you would think. If you Google it, you'll find there are many cases of someone suing or being otherwise concerned about copying, but then they find it can't possibly be the case. There was one with *Harry Potter*, I think . . . another wizard with glasses and a scar, but –'

'They definitely nicked it,' Hannah said. 'That's probably the only reason they wanted to do the film in the first place. To ruin it for us.'

'Well that can't be true,' Ms Guyomar said, 'because –' she stopped '– well, it just can't be true.'

'So what are we going to do?' Kitty said. 'We can't both do the same thing.'

'Can you show me what you have so far?' Ms Guyomar asked.

'Not really,' Kitty said. She didn't think a few photos found online would help their case.

'Well since the other group has actually made a start on their film . . .' Ms Guyomar gestured at Mackenzie, Amber and Louis. 'I'm afraid you're going to have to come up with a new idea.'

16

'I can't believe they did that,' Kitty said. 'I can't believe they just took our idea.'

It was lunchtime and she was sitting with Sunny and Hannah in one of the new outdoor relaxation areas: six red squashy chairs on a square of fake grass. Following the renovation, the school had almost as many areas for relaxation as it did for actual work.

'I can,' Hannah said. 'We should have thought of it actually. It's exactly Mackenzie's style. She wants the credit, but she never wants to do any work. Remember when she got done for copying in geography?'

'They didn't know that for sure though, did they?' Kitty said. 'It could have been a mistake.'

Hannah shrugged. 'I bet she did it. And she'll love winding me up too.'

'Cos of Louis,' Kitty said. 'But . . . I mean, he's with her now, so . . .'

'So she gets to gloat,' Hannah said, fiddling with her phone.

'I never thought someone would steal my notebook,' Sunny said. She'd been picking at the skin around her nails since they'd left Ms Guyomar's class. Kitty reached over and pulled one of her hands away. When they'd had the SATs, Sunny had made all of her fingers bleed. She'd come into the exams with plasters on every single one.

'Did they steal it though, Sunny?' Hannah asked. 'Or did you leave it somewhere? In the canteen maybe?'

Sunny shook her head. 'I think one of them must've taken it out of my bag. I can't believe Ms Guyomar's letting them get away with it.'

'I would've thought you'd be more careful with it, that's all,' Hannah said.

'Don't blame me,' Sunny said. 'How was I supposed to know they didn't have any ideas of their own? And what am I meant to do? Guard my bag all the time?'

'Yes,' Hannah said. 'You should guard your bag all the time. Because now what are we going to do?'

'It's not Sunny's fault, Han,' Kitty said.

'You were looking very cosy with Louis when we

walked in,' Sunny said, ignoring Kitty. 'What's all that about?'

Hannah rolled her eyes. 'We were the first there, that's all. Nothing suspicious about it. But anyway, he's all right when Mackenzie's not around.'

'Hmm,' Sunny said.

'There's nothing going on!' Hannah said. 'I wouldn't lie to you about something like that.'

Kitty's stomach flipped. They wouldn't think she would lie to them about something like that either, but she had. She thought again about telling them that Dylan was a girl, not a boy. That she liked girls, not boys. But she just couldn't do it. She'd only been out with Dylan once anyway, and she didn't even know if she was going to see her again. If she did – if she saw her again – then she'd tell them. Definitely.

'We just have to think of a new idea,' Sunny said. 'A better one.'

'I liked the idea we had,' Kitty said.

'Me too,' Hannah said. 'I don't think I can even be bothered to do it now. Let them have it if they want it so much.'

Kitty felt the same way. She'd be much happier keeping out of Mackenzie's way and out of any sort of spotlight altogether. She thought about the way she'd felt when she saw Amber at the festival and imagined that feeling multiplied by everyone in the school. It didn't bear thinking about.

'Just think of the money,' Sunny said.

'I don't need the money,' Hannah said, shrugging. 'I've got my mum's card details.'

'I do,' Kitty said. Her dad had still been at work when she'd gone to bed last night. Plus she'd seen the electricity bill on the table and she knew Grace wanted to go on the school trip she'd mentioned. Kitty would love to be able to give her parents some money.

'Does your mum know you're using her card?' Sunny asked Hannah.

Hannah shook her head. 'She won't even notice.'

'She'll notice if you go to London on a film-making course, right?' Sunny said.

Hannah groaned. 'I don't know. She might just be glad of a couple of weeks alone with James. But, yeah, okay. If we can think of something good, I'm still in.'

'Did we have any other ideas?' Kitty said. 'Anything at all?'

'Nope!' Hannah said, leaning back over the red squish ball chair she was sitting on and touching her hands to the ground.

'I can get a new notebook . . .' Sunny said.

'Oh thank god,' Hannah said sarcastically, her blonde hair brushing the astroturf.

'What about interviewing someone for each decade?' Kitty said, ignoring her. 'We could just show a little bit of all of them talking about their favourite places over the years. Or something like that.'

Sunny pulled a face. 'It doesn't seem grabby enough. We need to do something better than they do . . . obviously.'

'Grace was asking me about it last night,' Kitty said. 'I was telling her about the original idea and she said we should get dressed up in olden times stuff and be in the old photos.'

Hannah laughed. 'She wants us to actually go back in time? Ambitious!'

'No,' Kitty said. 'You know that stupid photo we had taken in Whitby a couple of years ago?'

It was a Victorian-style portrait they'd had done in a studio. They were all in Victorian clothes – their dad and Tom in top hats and waistcoats, Mum, Kitty and Grace in big dresses and hats. The photo was tea-coloured to make it look old and it made Kitty cringe every time she looked at it.

'Oh yeah,' Hannah said, grinning. 'We're not doing

that. I can get on board with time travel, but not embarrassing family photos.'

They sat in silence for a few moments. They could hear the school chickens clucking in their fancy modern coops on the other side of the playing field.

'Wait!' Sunny said. She closed her eyes and put her hands out in front of her, and Hannah and Kitty grinned at each other. One of the things Kitty liked the most about her friends was that they didn't hold a grudge. They could be snotty with each other and forget about it right away.

'That's it!' Sunny said, bouncing on her seat.

'We can't go back in time, Sun,' Hannah said. 'Unless you see a blue box anywhere around here?' She started singing the *Doctor Who* theme tune and Sunny shoved her.

'We film somewhere that hasn't changed,' Sunny said. 'And we're in old-fashioned clothes, right? We can get them from Miss Avison.'

Hannah and Kitty nodded.

'And we film it in black and white. And then it changes to present day and we film it in colour, make it look a bit livelier, but we're still in the old clothes, as if we've travelled from the past to present day St Margaret's!'

They all looked at each other.

'We could call it St Margaret's: Step into the Future,' Kitty said.

'Perfect!' Sunny said. 'Let's go and see Miss Avison after school.'

17

'I didn't know you had all this stuff!' Hannah said. 'Where did it come from?'

Kitty had been thinking the same thing. Who knew all of this was hidden away in a school store room? Twelve clothing rails. All crammed with vintage fashion.

Miss Avison shrugged. 'I've collected it all over the years. I did think about sorting through and getting rid of some during the renovation, but I just couldn't face it.'

'You shouldn't,' Kitty said. 'It's history.'

'It's beautiful,' Sunny sighed.

Miss Avison grinned. 'I'm glad to see you girls appreciate it. Sometimes students come in and complain about the dust and the smell. But how can you worry about the dust when there's this?' She held up a beige suede jacket with tassels dangling from underneath the sleeves. The girls all laughed.

'The eighties . . .' Miss Avison said. 'So what is it you need?'

'Something fifties?' Hannah said. 'I was thinking a prom dress, maybe?'

Miss Avison crossed the room and rolled a rack towards Hannah. 'Like the look of anything on here?' She glanced at Sunny.

'Don't worry,' Sunny said. 'I'm going to get my aunty to find me something.'

'A sari?'

'Yes. There's a photo in the hall of my nanu and her sisters, and they look so gorgeous. I'm going to try to get something like that.' Sunny had said the same to Hannah and Kitty on the way. They both knew the photo she meant; they'd seen it on the wall.

'Oh good,' Miss Avison said. 'I'd hate you to feel left out.'

Sunny turned away from the teacher and rolled her eyes at Kitty.

'Look at this!' Hannah said. She held out a bright pink prom dress with white flowers embroidered on the hem. 'Gorgeous!'

'It's very you,' Kitty said. 'But not very me . . .'

'Did you say the video's going to be black and white and then turning into colour?' Miss Avison asked. 'Because then you'll need clothes that are going to look just as good in both. Some colours look dull in black and white.'

'But . . .' Sunny said, 'it'll be in black and white, so . . .'

Miss Avison laughed. 'Yes, sorry, I didn't explain that very well. I mean some colours show up better on black-and-white film than others do. They look sharper, rather than different shades of grey. So you want clothes that will work for both parts of the video. Red is good.' She pulled out a red and white spotty dress and handed it to Hannah. 'And what about you, Kitty?'

Kitty pulled a face. 'I don't really wear dresses . . .'

'But you're going to have to for the video,' Hannah said.

'Not necessarily,' Miss Avison said. 'Just wait there . . .'

She crossed the room, started rummaging through the drawers of an enormous chest and came back with white trousers and a black top.

'Just to give you an idea,' she said, handing them to Kitty. 'I can have a look for something better if you like them. Very Doris Day.'

*

Hannah started pulling off her uniform as soon as they walked into her house after school.

'My eyes!' Sunny said.

'Oh don't be so repressed,' Hannah said. She balled up her shirt and stuck it straight into the washing machine. 'It's nothing you haven't seen in the changing rooms for PE.'

'I don't have to look when we're at school, do I?' Sunny said. 'Here you're all up in my face.'

'When will your mum be home, Han?' Kitty asked, just for something to say.

She'd already started worrying about the changing rooms at school and about her friends getting undressed in front of her. That would act differently once they knew she liked girls, wouldn't it? People at school would probably complain and she'd end up having to get changed in a side room by herself or something. And Hannah and Sunny would pretend to be cool, but then casually take themselves off to the bathroom to change. Tom once told her he used to wear his PE kit under his uniform, but he still had to get changed after and he hated it.

'Not for ages,' Hannah said. 'Last night it was ten.'

'So what did you do for your dinner?' Sunny asked.

Hannah shrugged. 'I was going to make pasta but I

couldn't be bothered so I just had cereal.' She crossed the kitchen and pointed at a note on the fridge. 'Look at this.'

Kitty and Sunny followed her over. The note said: *Collect dry cleaning, buy washing-up liquid, book car in for MOT?* Hannah had written, *I'm not your secretary!* underneath it.

'So you didn't do any of it then?' Kitty asked.

Hannah shook her head. 'She's got an actual secretary at work. Why doesn't she get her to do it?'

Kitty frowned. She couldn't really imagine not wanting to help her parents out. Even though she was annoyed that they were leaving her out of the loop with the MS, she still wanted to help whenever she could. Hannah and her mum used to be close too – it was just the two of them, after all – it was so sad that that could happen.

'It wouldn't be so bad,' Hannah said, 'if she spent any time with me when she's not so busy, you know? I get that she's got a really important job and I know that she loves it and she can't be here in the week. But then you'd think she'd want to spend weekends with me, wouldn't you? But she doesn't. Unless James can come too.'

'Is he still trying to be your friend?' Sunny said.

Hannah nodded. 'But I've told him, I don't need

any more friends. I've got you two. Now get your kit off, Kitty, and try your costume on.'

Hannah took the prom dress out of her bag and pulled it on. It fitted her perfectly, the straps sitting straight on her shoulders and the skirt flaring out perfectly from her waist.

'What do you think?' she said, twirling.

'Perfect,' Sunny said. 'The colour really suits you. Looks great with your hair.'

Kitty stepped into the cropped trousers Miss Avison had given her under her school skirt, before letting the skirt drop to the floor, then she picked it up and hung it over the back of a dining chair. She took off her school shirt and pulled the top over her head.

Hannah pretended to wolf-whistle, but Kitty knew she didn't look anywhere near as good as her friend. The trousers were too tight and the top was actually a little bit big – it was meant to be off-the-shoulder, but the shoulders kept slipping down so far Kitty's bra was showing.

'Doesn't really fit,' Kitty said. She looked down at herself trying to get an idea of how she looked.

'It looks good though,' Sunny said. 'When you make it the right size, it'll look great.'

'Is there a mirror down here?' Kitty asked.

Hannah shook her head. 'I'll take a photo on my phone.'

Kitty tried not to look too self-conscious while Hannah took the photo, then Hannah handed her the phone, saying, 'I'm starving. Anyone want a biscuit?'

Kitty looked at the photo. So much for not looking self-conscious. Her shoulders were hunched over and she looked scared and slightly gormless. She pulled her shoulders back. She was going to have to do better than that if she wasn't going to totally humiliate herself in the video. The outfit looked okay though. Bit boring, but that was fine. She didn't want to stand out, and with Hannah in a prom dress and Sunny in a sari, there was no chance of that. She wished she could be effortlessly stylish like Dylan, but she was happy to settle for not looking like a complete dork.

She pressed the screen to delete the photo – no point saving it, she only wanted to see what she looked like in the clothes – but once it had gone the previous photo came up. Kitty blinked at it. It was a selfie of Hannah and Louis – their faces pressed together, both of them grinning. It didn't look like an old one. Kitty glanced up to check that neither Hannah or Sunny was looking at her. They weren't: Hannah was rummaging in a cupboard and Sunny was sitting at the dining table, writing in her notebook. Kitty swiped to the previous photo, which she knew Hannah had taken last week at the bandstand. So the Louis photo was more recent . . . Kitty noticed a leafy branch in the top right-hand corner of the photo. Had that one been taken in the park too? On the same day?

She locked the phone and put it down on the dining table. What was Hannah doing?

18

Kitty was looking at photos of Doris Day online when Dylan phoned.

'Hey,' Dylan said.

For a moment, Kitty couldn't speak. She'd been worrying about what Dylan must have thought when she freaked out over Amber and wondering if she should have phoned to explain. She should have known Dylan wouldn't have been fazed.

'Hi,' Kitty squeaked finally. She cleared her throat and tried again. 'Sorry. Hi.'

'What are you up to?' Dylan said.

'Nothing much. School, you know,' Kitty said. 'We got costumes for the film today. Mine's a bit boring, but that's okay.'

'I didn't know you were wearing costumes,' Dylan said.

'Oh yeah, we weren't meant to be. The other group stole our idea.' Kitty scrolled through Pinterest's Doris

Day photos as she told Dylan what Louis, Mackenzie and Amber had done and the new idea they'd come up with.

'It sounds so cool,' Dylan said. 'Better than the first one even.'

'I hope so,' Kitty said, smiling.

'When are you filming?' Dylan asked. 'Can I come and watch?'

The back of Kitty's neck prickled with fear. 'I'm not sure yet, sorry. I can let you know though.'

'Oh, okay,' Dylan said.

Kitty felt guilty at how relieved she was. And then guilty again that she still hadn't told Hannah and Sunny. But she'd promised herself she'd tell them when she heard from Dylan again and she hadn't. Until now.

'Don't forget though,' Dylan said. 'I want to see your costume. What is it?'

'Just a white top and cropped black trousers,' she told Dylan. 'The teacher said it's very Doris Day, so I'm just looking at photos of her online now.'

'Ooh, I love Doris Day,' Dylan said. 'She's fantastic in *Calamity Jane*.'

'I think I saw that with Gran years ago. Does she fall in the mud?'

'Yep. And then she gets a makeover and she's all girly in a big yellow frilly dress.'

'I'm not wearing a frilly dress,' Kitty said.

'You should,' Dylan said. 'And a bonnet.'

Kitty laughed. 'I don't think that's quite the look we're going for.'

'How about a headscarf?' Dylan asked.

'I hadn't thought of that,' Kitty said. 'I don't know if I could pull it off.'

'You totally could,' Dylan said. 'Are you online now? Search "Doris Day headscarf".'

Kitty did, but there was still nothing she'd actually wear. In the first couple of pictures the actress had the scarf tied under her chin like a rain hood.

'Try "fifties headscarf",' Dylan said. 'Or I could just email you some photos. I love that look.'

Fifties headscarf was definitely better. As Kitty scrolled down the page, she found there were a few she could see herself wearing.

'A red and white spotty one would be good,' she told Dylan. 'Hannah's wearing a red spotty dress.'

'Ooh!' Dylan said. 'You could be Rosie the Riveter!'

'I'm Googling . . .' Kitty said.

The screen filled with illustrations of a woman wearing a denim shirt and spotted red headscarf, holding her arm up with her fist clenched and 'We Can Do It!' coming from a speech bubble above her head, along with some parodies of the same picture.

'She was originally representing the women working during World War Two while the men were off fighting,' Dylan said. 'But now she's a feminist icon. I love her. I think you'd look brilliant.'

'That's perfect,' Kitty said. 'Thank you.'

'Actually,' Dylan said, 'I've got a red spotty scarf you can borrow, if you want?'

'Oh, yes,' Kitty said. 'Please. If that's okay?'

'I could bring it to your house.' Dylan said. 'Tomorrow? After school?'

Kitty could hear the smile in Dylan's voice, but the thought of bringing Dylan home – introducing her to her parents, introducing her to Grace – made her feel even more panicky than the thought of telling Hannah and Sunny. What was wrong with her?

'The thing is . . . Mum's not really well enough,' Kitty said. 'My parents don't really want us to have friends round.'

'Oh,' Dylan said. 'I didn't know your mum was ill. I'm sorry.'

Kitty realised she hadn't even told Dylan about her mum. It was weird. She thought about Dylan so much, had so many imaginary conversations with her in her head, that it was hard to remember what was real and what wasn't.

'Sorry,' Kitty said. 'I forgot I hadn't told you. She's got multiple sclerosis.' Even though Kitty had talked about it with her friends and her gran, her throat still closed up as she said the words. Her mum had been better since she got the antidepressants. A bit better. But Kitty had hoped for more.

She heard Dylan blow out a breath. 'I'm sorry,' she said. 'I don't know what that is. I remember your gran saying that's what she wanted the charity to be this year . . .'

'Yeah,' Kitty said. 'That was why. It's to do with the central nervous system. I've read about it, but I can't remember all the details. Basically, it means she's been having loads of problems with her legs and it affects her hands too. There's different things that can happen. It's really horrible.'

'It sounds horrible,' Dylan said. 'So is she in hospital?'

'No, she's here. It can come and go – she can feel okay and then have a relapse. So we're waiting for it to go away really. She's been depressed, but she seems to be better. It's scary for Grace though – she doesn't understand. And she's worried she's going to . . . you know . . .'

'It's okay,' Dylan said. 'You don't need to say. It must be really hard for you. All of you.'

Kitty held the phone harder against her ear and closed her eyes. She wanted to pretend Dylan was here with her. She wished she lived nearer.

'It's just not fair, you know?'

'I know,' Dylan said.

Kitty could hear breathing, but she wasn't even sure if it was her own or Dylan's.

'I'm sorry,' Dylan said after a few seconds. 'I don't know what to say. I'm rubbish at this. We should talk about something else. Something stupid. What's your favourite colour?'

Kitty moved from the desk to the bed and flopped back against her pillows as she and Dylan talked about their favourite colours and favourite foods, the TV shows they remembered from when they were little, their favourite subjects at school. Dylan told Kitty about her mum – she worked in PR for a restaurant chain – and Kitty told Dylan about Grace and Tom. Kitty wanted to talk about Sunny and Hannah – so many of her favourite stories included them – but she didn't want Dylan to ask about meeting up with them. She wanted Dylan to herself for a bit longer.

After a while, Dylan said, 'Gah, I'm going to have to go. Mum's back and she's brought a takeaway.'

'Oh okay,' Kitty said. 'I should probably be making dinner actually. I didn't realise the time.'

'No, I know,' Dylan said. 'We've been talking for ages.'

Kitty pulled her legs up and hugged her knees against her chest. She didn't want to hang up.

'Always ring me if you're upset, okay?' Dylan said. 'I mean, you can ring me whenever you want, but if you're upset and you want to talk . . .'

Kitty nodded, even though Dylan couldn't see her. She wanted to. She wanted to be able to ring her. Always ring her. Whether she was upset or not. She wanted Dylan to understand everything about her and she wanted to understand everything about Dylan. But the thought of it was scary.

'I know I said you can't come here, but can we meet somewhere?' Kitty said. She closed her eyes and rested her forehead on her knees.

'Definitely,' Dylan said. 'What about the art college in Central Park? It's close to the ferry and not far from your house, right?'

'Um, yeah,' Kitty lied.

'We have some classes there and the Rec — the café — is great.'

The art college was in an enormous old building in a park on the other side of town. It was actually about twenty minutes walk from where Kitty lived — where she really lived, not where she'd told Dylan she lived — and perfect because none of her friends ever went there, as far as she knew.

'Great. So I'll meet you there at about four?'

'Okay,' Kitty said, her stomach already fluttering in anticipation. 'Whereabouts?'

'In the Rec?' Dylan said. 'I'll be the one with the spotty red scarf.'

19

Kitty walked through the gates of the park and up the wide path to the art college, feeling the mixture of excitement and fear she usually associated with rollercoasters. Or getting on a plane, back when they'd been able to afford holidays. Her stomach was fluttering with nerves, but at the same time she couldn't keep the smile off her face. This place was so intimidatingly cool anyway and then there was Dylan . . .

At the top of the steps, Kitty took a deep breath and pushed open the double doors to the foyer with its paintings and high ceilings and marble floor. She'd been here once before with school years ago, but she'd forgotten just how imposing it was. She couldn't really imagine coming here for college – what would that be like – to walk through those doors every day and know you were going to spend the day creating things, doing something you loved doing?

The Rec was tucked away in the back right-hand corner of the ground floor and Kitty headed straight there, skirting around an art installation that sort of looked like a game of Jenga made of sponges and bricks.

At the door, Kitty paused again and told herself to relax. It was just Dylan. She liked Dylan. Dylan liked her.

Kitty saw Dylan as soon as she walked in. She was sitting in the corner on the wide ledge of one of the enormous windows. She was wearing a pinafore overall, with the scarf tied to one of the straps, and cherry-red DMs and she was laughing. Because she wasn't alone. Three people were sitting at the small table next to the window. They were looking at Dylan and laughing too. Kitty thought about turning around and going straight back out, but then Dylan looked over and spotted her. She looked so happy to see her that Kitty couldn't stop herself smiling back.

Dylan hopped down from the window and crossed the room, steering around the tables and chairs while still looking at Kitty.

'Hey,' she said when she got to her.

For a second, Kitty thought Dylan was going to kiss her and she felt panic course through her. It must have shown on her face, because Dylan briefly looked surprised, but then smiled again. 'I'm sorry my friends are still here,' she said quietly. 'I thought they'd have left by now, but I accidentally mentioned you were coming and they wanted to meet you . . .'

'That's okay,' Kitty said. Even though it was more 'terrifying' than 'okay'.

'They're really nice, honestly,' Dylan said.

Dylan was right – they *were* really nice.

Charlie had a freckled face, turned-up nose and quiffed blonde hair. He ran an art club at Dylan's school and was, Dylan told Kitty, responsible for the Jenga installation in the foyer.

'Oh I saw that,' Kitty said. 'Cool.'

'Did you understand it?' Charlie said. 'The point of it, I mean?'

'Um . . .' Kitty said. 'I'm sorry, I didn't really stop to look; I just passed it.'

Charlie sighed. 'This is the problem. People just walk past and don't even look.'

'Sorry,' Kitty said.

'He's just joking,' Dylan told her. 'He likes to pretend he's a suffering artist, but he only did it for a coursework mark.'

'So, er, what *is* the point of it?' Kitty said.

'Apart from the mark?' Charlie said, fiddling with his phone. 'It's meant to represent how unbalanced life is. Some of it is brick and some is sponge and if you build your bricks on sponge –'

'It all falls down,' the girl Dylan had introduced as Sharda interrupted. 'This is what he claims,' she told Kitty, 'but really I think he got desperate and looked around the Rec for inspiration.' She pointed to a shelf of games in the corner. Jenga was on the very top.

'I did consider a full-sized Kerplunk first,' Charlie admitted. 'To represent how often in life everything's going well and then someone pulls out a stick and all your marbles fall out.'

Kitty laughed. 'I think I'm experiencing that at the moment.'

'Right?' Charlie said, grinning at her. 'Perfect metaphor for being a teenager.'

The other girl at the table, Olivia, said, 'You should do a series. Life represented through board games.'

Charlie squinted at the games shelf. 'Buckaroo? They'd never let me bring a donkey in.'

'Don't think Operation's going to work either,' Dylan said.

'Mousetrap!' Kitty said, spotting the game she'd

always wanted, but never got. 'You could do a full size one with people.'

Charlie nodded. 'I like that idea. I'm picturing Mr Grant in the little cage at the end . . .'

'He's Charlie's art teacher,' Dylan told Kitty. 'They have a love/hate relationship.'

'It's hate/hate today,' Charlie said. 'Actually, I'm reconsidering that Operation idea . . .'

By the time Charlie had finished telling them all the things his teacher had done to annoy him that day, Sharda and Olivia said they had to go and Charlie decided to go with them and get on with the homework he'd just insisted he wasn't going to do.

The three of them left in a flurry of bags and coats, hugs for Dylan and friendliness to Kitty.

'Sorry,' Dylan said, once they'd left. 'I didn't think they'd hang around. They don't usually.'

Kitty smiled. 'It's okay. They were great.'

'They are. But you weren't expecting a big Meeting the Friends thing and I haven't met your friends, so . . .'

Kitty bit the inside of her cheek. 'You can though,' she said. 'Soon.'

'Oh yeah?' Dylan said, smiling.

Kitty nodded. 'I've told them about you. They want to meet you.' She wasn't lying, she told herself.

She had told them and they did want to meet Dylan. They just thought she was a boy. There was no way she could tell Dylan that though, not when she'd so casually introduced Kitty to her own friends.

Kitty frowned. She could fix the other lie, at least.

'I need to tell you something,' she said, fiddling with a sugar packet someone had left on the table. 'I don't live where I said I live.'

Dylan looked confused. 'What do you mean?'

'I don't live up here near the ferry. I live at the other end of town. Near school. My school.'

'So . . . why did you say you did?'

'Because I wanted to walk along the prom with you,' Kitty said. She put her hands up to her hot cheeks.

Dylan shook her head. 'Wait, what?'

Kitty cringed. 'When you saw me throwing stones into the river? And then we walked along to the ferry?'

'Yeah, I know.'

'Well I just wanted to walk with you, so I pretended I was walking home too.'

Dylan grinned at her. 'That is so sweet.'

'It's not,' Kitty said through her fingers. 'It's sad.'

Dylan reached over and pulled Kitty's hands down from her face. 'It's not sad. It's lovely. Thank you.'

Dylan had obviously scooted her chair closer to reach Kitty's hands because she was much closer than she had been. Kitty looked down at Dylan's lips. She wanted to kiss her. But she knew she couldn't do it. What if Dylan didn't want to kiss her? How humiliating would that be? There was no one else in the café – apart from the skinny girl with blue hair behind the counter – but even so, if Kitty kissed Dylan and Dylan stopped her she would die of shame.

'Do you want to kiss me?' Dylan whispered. Her eyes were twinkling and she looked like she was about to laugh.

Kitty thought about saying no. She worried that Dylan was laughing at her. But she really, really wanted to kiss Dylan. So she nodded. But when she still didn't make a move to kiss Dylan, Dylan kissed her instead.

20

'I can't believe you walked me to the ferry and then pretended you lived there!' Dylan said for about the fifth time. They were sitting on a bench next to the pond in the park. Dylan was pressed right up against Kitty, holding her hand. She'd been holding her hand, in fact, pretty much constantly since they'd kissed.

'I didn't know what else to say!' Kitty said.

'You could have said, "I just want to walk with you."'

Kitty shook her head. 'Maybe *you* could say that. I couldn't.'

'But you knew I liked you!'

'But I wasn't sure you liked me . . . like that.'

'Like this?' Dylan said and kissed Kitty again.

And like the last time − the first time − Kitty's insides melted. She felt like she could melt right off − or through − the bench. She felt like she was dreaming, but at the same time she felt more awake than she'd ever been. She felt like she wanted to keep doing this forever, but also like she should jump up, run home and never do anything like this again. It was all very confusing.

'Is it okay to do this here?' she said, once the kissing had stopped. Maybe it wasn't something she should be doing on a bench in public where anyone could see them. And tell her parents. Or her friends.

'Why not?' Dylan said.

'With, you know, people around?'

Dylan shook her head. 'Does it matter?'

'No,' Kitty said. 'I just . . . I think I'd feel better somewhere a bit more private.'

Dylan stared at her and Kitty stared back. Dylan's fringe was hanging over one eye and Kitty wished she could reach out and push it to the side, so she could see Dylan's eyes more clearly. The one she could see crinkled at the corner and Kitty automatically smiled back.

'Come with me,' Dylan said.

Kitty stood up. 'Where to?'

'It might not still be here, but when I used to come here when I was little – my nan and granddad lived over the other side . . . in Somerville, you know – there was this tree . . . There it is!'

She pointed to a tree just slightly back from the edge of the pond.

It was a weeping willow or something like that. Branches and leaves that reached all the way down to the ground like the skirt of a leafy ballgown.

Kitty followed Dylan over and they pulled the branches apart and walked through. Inside, the sun was slanting through the branches, creating patterns of light on the grass.

'Oh wow!' Kitty said.

'It's magical, isn't it?' Dylan sat down, leaning back against the tree's thick trunk. 'I wanted to live here when I was little. I used to bring stuff with me and hide it. Did you ever read *The Magic Faraway Tree*?'

Kitty nodded.

'I was sure this was it and that one day Moonface would pop down and invite me up.'

Kitty looked up at the tree. It was perfect. Dylan was perfect. She sat down next to her.

'Better?' Dylan asked. 'More private.'

'I'm sorry,' Kitty said. 'I know I should be . . . I shouldn't worry about what people think, I just –'

'No, you shouldn't.' Dylan picked at the nail varnish on her thumb. 'Sorry. I mean, I know it's hard at first. It takes some getting used to. For you and everyone else.'

'Were you okay with it? And your family?'

'I pretty much knew before I knew it was a thing,' Dylan said, smiling. 'Mum says I talked about girls from when I was really young. I remember one of my friends saying she liked a boy and I thought that was really weird. Like, "A boy? Why?!"' She grinned at Kitty.

'I just wasn't sure,' Kitty said. 'I thought maybe ... that I just wasn't ready for boys. And maybe I was kidding myself that I liked girls. But I always thought about girls more than boys. I always had crushes on girls.'

'At school?'

'Everywhere. At school and, yeah, like celebrities? I remember my gran had this magazine and there was a photo of Billie Piper? It was a paparazzi photo and it wasn't glamorous or ... sexy or anything, but I couldn't stop looking at it. I kept sneaking looks at it all the time I was at her house. I asked her if I could have it and I cut the picture out and had it in the back of my diary.'

Dylan grinned. 'Have you still got it?'

Kitty nodded.

'Billie Piper is hot,' Dylan said.

They held hands as they walked back to the ferry.

Kitty kept looking down at her fingers entwined with Dylan's. She couldn't quite believe it. Dylan kept grinning at her.

'You're so funny.'

'It's okay for you,' Kitty said. 'You've had a girlfriend before. This is all new to me.'

'It's kind of new to me, too,' Dylan said, swinging their hands out between them. 'Tilda wasn't really into PDAs.'

Tilda, Kitty thought. So Elaine's granddaughter was Matilda, not Maisie or Martha.

'Really?' Kitty said.

Dylan shook her head. 'She said it wasn't anyone else's business. Which, you know, it isn't. But if you're happy . . .'

Kitty grinned at her. She was happy. Really happy. So happy that she felt like skipping. Like laughing out loud. Like grabbing Dylan and kissing her and not worrying whether anyone saw or not. Instead she just pulled her closer and bumped her with her arm. Dylan kissed her cheek.

They crossed the road to the ferry terminal and stopped, looking up at the clock.

'So when will I see you again?' Dylan asked. 'Did you find out when you're filming yet?'

161

Kitty shook her head. 'Not yet, no. I'll ring you, though.'

'Good,' Dylan said.

They stood facing each other, both smiling.

'I'd better not miss my ferry,' Dylan said.

'I need to get home anyway.' Kitty said.

'Your real home this time?' Dylan grinned.

Kitty reached out and grabbed Dylan's hand again. She stepped closer and looked at her mouth. The corners of Dylan's lips quirked in a smile and Kitty leaned forward and kissed her.

'Thank you,' Kitty said.

'What for?'

Kitty shook her head. 'I'll phone you.'

Dylan grinned again and turned to walk down the ramp to the ferry. Kitty watched her go, waiting for her to turn and wave before she disappeared out of sight. She couldn't stop smiling. Her stomach was so fluttery it was almost painful, but it was a good kind of pain. It made her want to laugh out loud. Dylan turned and waved, and Kitty waved back before turning the corner to the prom. Which is when she saw Sam.

She knew immediately that he'd seen her kissing Dylan. She could tell by the look on his face. He looked shocked and confused and was practically opening and closing his mouth like a fish.

'Sam,' Kitty said. She couldn't think. She could hear a sound like wind rushing in her ears.

'Hey,' he said.

Kitty couldn't get over the look on his face. She didn't know Sam that well, shouldn't care what he thought, but she was already picturing that same look on Hannah's face, on Sunny's, on everyone at school and it made her want to run right out of her life.

She shook her head. 'It's not what you think,' she said. 'I mean . . . it's not what it looks like.'

'You don't have to –' Sam started to say.

Kitty held her hands up in front of her. 'No, honestly. It's nothing. That girl . . . I'm not gay.'

Sam opened his mouth to speak, but before he said anything Kitty saw his eyes get wide and she knew. She turned round.

'I forgot to give you this,' Dylan said. She was holding out the scarf.

21

'You okay?' Sam said.

Once her brain had managed to communicate with the rest of her body, Kitty had run back round the corner after Dylan, but Dylan was already out of sight.

Kitty leaned on the railings and looked out at the river. Her skin felt raw, like she had sunburn. She couldn't speak.

'I only came over for this,' Sam said.

Kitty looked round to see he had one foot resting at the side of a football.

'It rolled across the road,' he said. 'I wasn't . . . I didn't mean to . . . you know. I don't actually stalk you, honest.'

Kitty nodded. 'It doesn't matter,' she said, but she wasn't sure if it was actually loud enough for him to hear.

'You like her, eh?' Sam said. He'd moved next to her, his elbows on the railings.

Kitty scraped at a loose bit of paint with a fingernail. Her hands were shaking.

'She's hot,' Sam said.

Kitty looked at him. He grinned.

'What I said . . .' she said. 'That was rubbish. I am gay.'

'Yeah,' he said. 'I got that.'

Kitty blew out her breath. 'You're sort of the first person I've said that to.'

Sam looked surprised. 'You haven't told Sunny? Or Hannah?'

Kitty shook her head. 'No. Keep putting it off. Too scared.'

They both watched as the ferry pulled out from the terminal. Dylan was on that boat, Kitty thought. What was she thinking? The look on Dylan's face flashed through Kitty's mind. She was hurt. And disappointed. And angry. The paint chip Kitty was picking at stuck painfully under her nail.

'Text her,' Sam said. 'Say sorry.'

Kitty shook her head.

'Go on.' Sam bumped her shoulder with his. 'Tell her you thought I'd tell everyone at school and you're not up for that yet.'

Kitty's stomach lurched violently. 'You won't, will you? Tell anyone?'

Now Sam looked hurt and disappointed. 'Course not. You should, though.'

'Yeah,' Kitty said. 'Maybe.'

Once the ferry was halfway across – closer to Dylan's side than Kitty's – she and Sam set off walking along the prom towards home.

Sam didn't pick the ball up; he just somehow managed to keep it rolling just in front of his feet the whole time. Kitty watched it as much as she could without walking into something or tripping over. It was sort of hypnotic.

'This is me,' Sam said when they were about halfway back to Kitty's. He pointed up Grant Road. Kitty hadn't known he lived up there. She went to a dentist there, when she was little.

'Okay,' Kitty said. 'Thanks.'

'Thanks for ruining everything?' Sam said, raising one eyebrow.

Kitty shook her head. 'No, that was me. Thanks for walking back with me. And, you know, for what you said.'

'No probs,' Sam said. 'See ya.'

He booted the football against the opposite wall and crossed to meet it, but then turned and walked back to Kitty as the ball rolled back.

'Is Sunny seeing anyone?' he blurted. He was actually blushing.

'Sunny?' Kitty said.

'Yeah.' Sam bent down and picked the ball up, holding it against his stomach. 'I mean, I don't know if she does. Go out. I've never heard that she's seeing anyone or anything. But I, uh, like her, so I just thought I'd ask.'

'She's not allowed,' Kitty said. 'Her parents won't let her have a boyfriend or anything. But I can talk to her . . .'

Sam grinned. 'Yeah?'

Kitty nodded. She could totally imagine Sunny with Sam.

Sam dropped the football and dribbled it across the road. Kitty had just set off walking again when she heard him shout her name. She turned.

'Text her!' he yelled.

Kitty nodded, waved, and kept walking.

As soon as Kitty opened the front door she knew something was wrong. And then she realised her dad's car had been outside and it shouldn't have been. He was supposed to be at work.

'Dad?' she called.

'Kitty?' Grace appeared out of the kitchen. She looked pale and scared, her eyes were big and wide. She had a smear of something that looked like Nutella on her cheek.

'What's going on?' Kitty said. 'What's wrong?'

'Mum's really ill,' she said. 'I went in to see her when I got back from school and . . .' She started to cry and Kitty couldn't make out what she was saying. Kitty steered her back into the kitchen and sat her down at the table, holding her hand.

'Just breathe – it's okay,' Kitty said. 'I can't understand you when you're crying.'

Kitty reached for the glass of milk on the opposite side of the table and slid it over to Grace.

'I couldn't wake her up,' Grace managed to say.

'Oh my god,' Kitty said. Her eyes filled and she squeezed her little sister's hand. 'Is Dad with her now?'

Grace nodded.

Kitty wanted to go right up and find out what was happening, but she couldn't leave Grace. She shuffled her chair closer and put her arm round her sister.

Grace had stopped crying and finished her milk by the time their dad came down. Kitty hadn't asked her any more questions and Grace seemed sleepy and drained.

'What's wrong?' Kitty said, as soon as her dad walked in. He looked drained and pale too, and a tuft of his hair was sticking out above his ear.

'It's okay,' he said. 'Your mum's got a bit of a fever and it's –'

'Does she need to go to hospital?' Kitty asked. She wanted to stand up and hug her dad, but Grace was still leaning against her, one hand clinging to the edge of Kitty's school jumper.

Her dad shook his head. 'I've talked to the doctor. She said that sometimes a fever can bring out old symptoms.' He sat down at the end of the table next to Kitty. 'It could be that the nerve damage hadn't finished healing or that it just hasn't healed well enough.'

'So what are the symptoms?' Kitty said.

'Remember when she was first ill?' her dad said. 'And she couldn't get out of bed?'

Kitty nodded.

'And she's a bit . . . confused. That's why she –' He rubbed his face with both hands.

'She didn't know my name,' Grace said, against Kitty's shoulder.

Kitty shuddered. She put her arm around her sister. Poor Grace.

'You know it's because she's ill, though, Gracie,' their dad said. 'Right? You know sometimes when you've got a cold or the flu you get confused?'

Grace sat up straight, pulling away from Kitty. 'When I was sick at school that time, I called Mr George "Mummy".'

'Exactly,' their dad said, smiling at Grace. 'Your mum just needs to rest and get over this cold and then she'll be fine.'

Kitty picked up Grace's glass and tried to drink some milk, even though there were only a few drops left. It seemed like her parents were always telling her everything was going to be fine, but then it just never was.

22

'Action!'

Sunny's sister Aisha stood at the end of the pier with the camera Ms Guyomar had given them, and Kitty, Hannah and Sunny ran towards her. Kitty felt like a complete idiot. The pier wasn't busy – it was too early in the morning for that – but there were a couple of men fishing off the edge and a woman sitting on a bench reading the Sunday newspaper, so it was enough to make Kitty feel self-conscious. Plus she was wearing cropped trousers and a gingham top and she'd tied Dylan's red scarf in her hair. She did not feel like herself. At all.

Sunny, however, was hamming it up. Kitty had told her what Sam had said and even though she said she couldn't go out with him, she was still giddy just knowing he liked her. The fifties sari her aunty had found for her was absolutely gorgeous – bright turquoise with a fuller skirt than modern saris and covered with embroidery and beading. The scarf over one shoulder wrapped around her waist and she wore a matching headscarf.

Hannah looked fantastic in the prom dress and the most comfortable of all of them – it was the kind of thing she'd love to have the chance to wear more often. She took loads of selfies and Kitty couldn't help wondering if she was sending them to Louis.

'Can you go back and do it again?' Aisha said when they reached her. 'And this time, Kitty, try not to look like you're hating every minute of it.'

'But I am,' Kitty muttered, as the three of them walked back to the starting point, near the sun deck at the end of the pier.

'Cheer up, Kits,' Sunny said. 'The sun's shining, you've got us, and you only have to put up with Aisha bossing you about today – I've got her for my whole life.'

'And it'll be over soon.' Hannah tugged on the tied end of Kitty's scarf, which was actually Dylan's scarf.

Kitty hadn't been sure whether she should wear it – she'd texted Dylan saying sorry and Dylan had replied saying she'd call, but she hadn't yet. Kitty kept telling herself that it had only been two days, but she was terrified that she wouldn't call. Ever. And she still didn't know if she was brave enough to call Dylan herself. Not after what she'd done. She told herself she was giving her time, but she wasn't sure if that was true or if she was just waiting for her own courage to appear. It hadn't yet.

And she felt guilty to be spending so much time wondering and worrying about Dylan when her mum was ill. She was better than she had been – she was more awake than asleep now – but it meant her dad hadn't been able to work and she knew money was becoming a problem.

'Action!' Aisha shouted again.

This time, as they ran, the three of them holding hands, Aisha shouted encouragement that did actually make Kitty smile. When they'd almost reached her, she shouted 'Jump!' and they leapt in the air. The men fishing turned to look and the woman put her newspaper down and shielded her eyes to watch them. Kitty still felt like an idiot, but at least she was being an idiot with her friends.

'One more time!' Aisha said, looking down at the camera.

'I think your sister's just enjoying torturing us,' Hannah said. She pulled one of her shoes off and poked at the plaster on her heel. 'These things weren't made for running and jumping.'

'Just keep telling yourself this is the last one,' Sunny said. 'After this we can go and get ice cream and ignore Aisha for the rest of the day.'

As they walked back up the pier, the wooden planks creaking underfoot, Kitty's phone buzzed in her back pocket. Her stomach lurched before she even looked.

'Hang on a sec,' she said.

Peeling away from Hannah and Sunny, she walked over to the railing and took a deep breath before tapping the message icon. It was from Dylan. It just said: *Call me.*

'I just need to ring someone,' she shouted. She sounded slightly hysterical even to herself.

'Aisha needs to go soon,' Sunny called back. Then she grinned. 'Say hello to Dylan!'

Kitty tried to smile. 'I won't be long, I promise.'

She looked around for somewhere more private and half-ran back down the pier to the coffee shop near the sun deck. It wasn't yet open, but there was a man inside cleaning the windows. He winked at Kitty. She kept walking round to the front of the building and, once she knew she was alone, she tapped Dylan's name.

'Hey,' Dylan said, almost immediately.

Kitty's eyes filled with tears. 'I'm so, so sorry. I totally freaked out.'

'No, I know. I get it.' She didn't sound quite like herself. The Dylan Kitty knew so far. She sounded more serious. Sadder.

'The boy – Sam,' Kitty said. 'I told him straight away. I came after you, but you'd gone, but then I told him.'

'Yeah?' Dylan said. 'I saw you. From the ferry. By the railings.'

'Yes! I couldn't even think. I felt so terrible. I still do. I just . . .'

'This is new for you. And it's hard. I know. But it's hard for me too. I need to know that you want to be with me –'

'I do,' Kitty said. Her legs felt wobbly. She sat down on the floor, her back against the café.

'But I need to be in your life, too,' Dylan said.

'You are,' Kitty said. She stared down at her feet in the yellow Converse she'd worn to the festival. 'I'm wearing your scarf.' She pulled one of the ends across her face. It smelled like Dylan. Like fresh mint and mandarins. 'I wanted to have a bit of you with me.'

Dylan laughed and it was the first time Kitty felt like it might actually be okay.

'That's good,' Dylan said, 'but I don't want you to have a bit of me. I want you to have all of me. In your life, I mean. I want to meet your parents. I want to meet your friends. I want to come and watch you making the film.'

Kitty rested her head on her knees. 'We're doing it now. We've nearly finished.'

She heard Dylan sigh. 'I like you, Kitty, but I don't want to be your guilty secret.'

'I'll tell them,' she said. 'I promise.'

'Come on!' Aisha shouted, as Kitty walked back around the café. 'I've got to go in a minute. Just one more time.'

Kitty ran to the end of the pier, and Hannah and Sunny flung their arms around her, laughing and jumping up and down. She'd known them for so long and she loved them both so much.

She was going to tell them. She absolutely was. But not today.

23

Ms Guyomar had actually seated herself between Kitty, Hannah and Sunny, and Mackenzie, Louis and Amber, which Kitty thought was probably for the best. Kitty was happy with the new film, but she knew that Hannah and Sunny still resented the others for stealing the idea so it was probably best just to keep everyone apart. The hall was full and the noise level was high while Mr Ashford used the long hook thing to close the curtains against the sun that was slanting across the room and making the screen hard to see.

Kitty stared at the screen that scrolled down at the back of the stage. She'd seen it before, they all had – there'd been a presentation about the new school when they'd started – but the thought that their film was going to be shown up there, on that huge screen, in front of the entire school was making her feel beyond sick.

'I wish they'd get on with it,' Hannah whispered.

Kitty nodded, but she wasn't sure she agreed. The sooner it was shown, the sooner it would be over, yes, but she was still hoping for the last minute reprieve of a technology breakdown. Or the fire alarm. She shuffled on her uncomfortable folding chair.

Once the curtains were all closed and the hall was dark and Mrs Savage had shushed the students making 'Wooooooh!' noises, the screen lit up, showing the desktop of Ms Guyomar's laptop.

Kitty put her hand over her mouth. She felt Hannah lean against her and she leaned back. She wanted to look at her friends, to say they were in this together, but she didn't want to take her eyes off the screen.

'We have a very special presentation this morning,' Mrs Savage boomed from the edge of the stage. 'As some of you know, six of our students are taking part in the local council's film-making competition. Ms Guyomar assures me the films are wonderful and I for one am really looking forward to them.'

'Get on with it then,' a boy in the row behind muttered. Ms Guyomar turned around and shushed him.

'The first film,' Mrs Savage said, 'is by Hannah Coleman, Kitty Harrison and Sunny Ahmed and is called "Step into the Future".'

The screen filled with the title page Sunny had

made – St Margaret's in 'Wish You Were Here'-type script over a collage of old photos of the town. Sunny had used a website to make it look like a postcard.

'Enjoy!' Mrs Savage said, waving at the screen. She walked down the few steps from the stage and sat down at the end of the row.

Kitty put both hands on her stomach, which was churning violently. She thought the film was good – she really did – but what if she was wrong? This could be a disaster.

The video opened with a screenshot of Google Maps showing the map of St Margaret's, then the cursor moved across the screen, grabbed the little yellow person and pulled it over to the pier. But when the screen zoomed in, an old black-and-white photo of the pier appeared. It changed from a still to video – of Kitty, Sunny and Hannah walking down the pier in black and white and their fifties outfits – and then suddenly merged to colour as they ran towards the camera. People laughed, but Kitty thought it sounded like they actually thought it was funny, not that they were laughing at them.

As the short video ended, the words *St Margaret's: Step into the Future* filling the screen, people actually applauded.

Kitty's stomach was still churning, but she felt less terrified and more excited. She leaned forward to grin along the row at Sunny and Hannah who were both beaming.

There was some muttering and chair shuffling while everyone watched the cursor locating the file called 'St Margaret's: Best of Both Worlds'.

'I can't believe they even stole the title!' Hannah hissed in Kitty's ear.

Kitty shook her head.

People cheered – and some booed – as 'Best of Both Worlds' by Miley Cyrus started to play and then the film started. It was exactly what Kitty, Sunny and Hannah had discussed, and Sunny had planned in the missing notebook: black and white photos of 'old' St Margaret's alternating with clips of modern St Margaret's. It didn't look anywhere near as professional as Kitty, Sunny and Hannah's film and the music was jarring.

Kitty was just starting to relax when the screen filled with an old photo of Central Park – the pond near the art college – and it faded out to be replaced by a long-range film of the park taken more recently.

And then the camera zoomed in on two figures sitting on the bench.

Kitty's body seemed to know what was happening before her brain had quite worked it out. A feeling like pins and needles ran down both of her arms and into her hands, and she felt herself jolt back against her chair as if she actually had received an electric shock.

On the screen – the screen that took up most of the back wall of the hall, the screen that everyone in school was currently staring at – Kitty and Dylan were sitting together, close enough together that it was pretty obvious they weren't just friends, but just sitting together even so. But then Kitty laughed and turned towards Dylan and Dylan leaned forward and kissed her.

'What's on earth?!' Kitty heard Mrs Guyomar say.

Kitty couldn't see what was happening on the screen now – her eyes had filled with tears. She wanted to scream. She wanted to hit someone. She wanted to hide.

She stood up, one of her school shoes slipping slightly on the polished wooden floor. Someone – presumably Hannah – grabbed at her arm. Kitty shook her off and ran along the front row, up the side of the hall and out through the double doors. As she burst out into the foyer, she heard 'Best of Both Worlds' start to play again.

24

Kitty was halfway along the prom by the time she'd stopped sobbing. She'd never in her life walked out of school before, but she didn't even hesitate at the gate – she just had to get out. But now she wasn't sure where she should go. She stopped outside the park and leaned against the railings, looking across the river towards town. She thought about keeping going along the prom and getting the ferry over to see Dylan, but then she remembered Dylan was at school and someone else's school was the last place she wanted to go.

She couldn't go and see her anyway because she still hadn't told her friends. They knew, but she hadn't told them. Why hadn't she? She'd thought about it so much over the past couple of weeks. She wanted to tell them. They'd always talked about everything in the past, so why not this? It wasn't even that she thought they'd have a problem with it, not really. If she really thought they were homophobic she wouldn't be friends with them. So what was it?

She walked a bit further, thinking maybe she'd still get the ferry over and then get the bus to her gran's. Her gran would understand everything. She always did, always had. She'd sympathise, tell Kitty that Mackenzie, Amber and Louis were jealous and mean and not even worth worrying about. And she'd probably also have cake. But the thought of the forty-five minute journey made Kitty's heart sink.

She sat down on a bench, pulled her knees up to her chest and stared out at the water until her eyes teared up again.

She wasn't even that bothered about Mackenzie, Louis or Amber. She knew it wasn't even about her, not really. They'd just seen something too good not to share. School was like that. Amber must have seen her at the festival after all. She'd probably been wetting herself with excitement.

But what was school going to be like now? People muttering and sniggering behind her back? The thought of it made her feel sick.

But she kept coming back to the fact that none of this would have happened if she'd been braver. If she'd been open about who she was. That was the thing with Hannah and Sunny. No, they wouldn't have a problem with her being gay, but she'd still lied to them. There was no arguing with that. She hadn't just let them think Dylan was a boy – which would be bad enough – she'd actually told them she was. Why had she done that? She swung her legs down from the bench and tipped her face back up to the sun. Because she'd been scared, that was why.

By the time the sun had dried the tears on her face, she knew exactly who she wanted to talk to. She stood up and turned back down the prom towards home.

After kicking her shoes off in the hall, Kitty went straight up the stairs and pushed open her parents' bedroom door. The bed was empty, the duvet pulled back and the pillows bunched up. Panic leaped in Kitty's chest. Had her mum had to go to hospital? Last night she said she'd been feeling much better and Kitty had even sat with her for a little while, doing her homework.

And weird as it sounded, the room felt better. The windows were open, so open that the light breeze outside was blowing the curtains gently inside. The uncomfortable atmosphere Kitty had felt in there for the last few months had gone. She didn't feel like she needed to run straight out of the room. In fact, she almost wanted to climb into her parents' bed and cry herself to sleep, but instead she turned and ran back down the stairs.

Her mum wasn't in the kitchen, the lounge or in the small front room that they hardly ever used – it was supposed to be a proper dining room, but at the moment was acting as the junk room, full of all the stuff that didn't fit anywhere else in the house.

Confused, Kitty looked at the clock. It was 2pm, so her dad would still be driving for another hour until it was time to pick Grace up from school. So where was her mum? She ran back upstairs and checked the bathroom, but it was empty. As far as she knew, her mum hadn't gone out on her own since she got her diagnosis. Kitty felt the panic rising again. Where could she be?

Kitty had been standing in the kitchen for a couple of minutes, wondering if it would be an overreaction to phone her gran, when she noticed the back door was open. It wasn't wide open, but the wind made it move slightly. Kitty's first thought was that someone had broken in and kidnapped her mum, but then she mentally slapped herself and went out into their small back garden.

Her mum was sitting on a dining chair, her head back, face turned up to the sun, the John Grisham book Kitty had seen in her bedroom a few weeks ago open on her knee.

'Mum?' Kitty said.

Her mum shrieked and jumped, the book falling to the floor.

'Kitty! You scared me!'

Her long hair was tied up loosely and her face was pink, presumably from being in the sun after so long cooped up inside. She looked beautiful.

'Are you okay?' Kitty asked.

'I'm fine. Are you back from school already? What time is it?' She looked confused, but normal confused, the way she used to look when Kitty interrupted her when she was engrossed in a book and she had to pull herself back into the real world.

Kitty shook her head. 'No. I walked out of school. Something happened and I . . . I really need to talk to you.'

'Oh Kitty,' her mum said and held out her arms.

Kitty stepped right into them.

25

Kitty opened the door expecting to find her dad and Grace – she knew it was past the end of school – but she should have known it would be Hannah and Sunny.

They both looked sorry and worried and nervous and Kitty wanted to cry again at the sight of them.

'Are you okay?' Sunny said, picking at her fingers.

Kitty found she couldn't speak. She nodded, her eyes full of tears.

'We brought your bag, you daft cow,' Hannah said, throwing Kitty's school bag into the hall behind her. 'We came after you, but we got caught by Savage and she wouldn't let us leave.'

'Then Ms Guyomar told Mrs Savage that they had added the bit with you and she almost exploded,' Sunny said. 'You should have seen her. Turns out they were only doing the film because Savage made them. It was meant to be a character-building teamwork thing. She's furious.'

'So after that we tried to get out again and Mr Glass caught us that time,' Hannah said. 'It's worse than prison, that place.'

Kitty smiled at them through her tears.

Sunny reached over and grabbed Kitty's hand.

'Fancy a walk on the beach?' Hannah said.

'Did your mum know you were gay?' Sunny asked, as they clambered over the rocks to get to the sand.

Kitty shook her head. 'I don't think so. She didn't say so.'

'What did she say?' Hannah grabbed Kitty's arm as she slipped on some moss.

'She was amazing,' Kitty said. 'She said the most important thing to them is that I'm happy and safe.'

'I totally knew you were gay,' Hannah said, as they walked along the sand.

'You did not!' Kitty said. 'You're always trying to fix me up!'

Hannah laughed. 'Nah, I didn't. I mean, I wondered sometimes – you never liked any boys, but I thought that was just cos the boys here are so . . .' She pulled a horrified face. 'But I always thought that if you were then you would have told me . . . us. So I thought you probably weren't.'

'How long have you known?' Sunny asked.

Kitty kicked at some seaweed. 'I don't know really. I mean, I've thought . . . maybe, for a while. But I thought perhaps it was a phase or something.'

'Isn't that just something people say when they don't believe in people being gay?' Sunny said. 'I mean, did anyone ask Hannah if it was just a phase when she started going out with Louis? You know, "You like him now, but maybe you'll meet a nice girl?"'

'Or he will,' Hannah said. 'A horrible girl.'

Kitty frowned. 'Is something going on with you and Louis?'

Hannah looked startled. 'Way to change the subject!'

'No, I just . . . While we're getting things out in the open, I saw the photo on your phone.'

'What photo?' Sunny said.

Hannah groaned. 'He sent me an old photo of us. He said he wants to get back with me. Did you see it when we were trying on the costumes?'

Kitty nodded.

Hannah kicked one of the rocks towards the water. 'I wondered if you did.'

'I thought it was a new one,' Kitty said. 'I thought

you'd taken it in the park that day. When you went off to the loo and Mackenzie had a go at me.'

'You thought we took a bog selfie?!' Hannah said. 'Ugh, Kitty! No, it was an old one he texted me. And I saved it to my photos.'

'Not in the bog,' Kitty said. 'Outside the bog maybe.'

'Oh that's much better,' Hannah said, rolling her eyes.

'So are you going to get back with him?' Sunny asked.

Hannah bent down and picked up one of the pebbles, turning it over in her hands. 'I don't know. At first I was just going to mess with him, you know? To wind Mackenzie up. But then . . . I don't know. I like him.'

'But he cheated on you because you wouldn't do . . . stuff,' Kitty said.

Hannah pulled a face. 'Sort of. I might've exaggerated that a bit. I wasn't very nice to him.'

'You don't have to be nice to boys –' Sunny started.

'Not that like!' Hannah said. 'God! I just . . . I was a bit of a cow. I never rang him and I took the piss out of him in front of his friends.' She ran her hands back through her hair. 'I wanted to make sure he really liked me. That he wasn't just interested in . . . you know.'

'I don't get it,' Sunny said. 'How would that prove he really liked you?'

Hannah groaned. 'If he kept going out with me anyway. It was a rubbish idea, I know.'

Sunny shook her head. 'Sometimes I'm glad I'm not allowed a boyfriend. I don't understand it at all.'

'I'm not saying it's right what he did,' Hannah said, 'but he's sorry. And he didn't know about the film, Kit. He says it was all Mackenzie and Amber.'

'So you're going to get back with him?' said Kitty.

'Maybe,' Hannah said. 'I haven't decided yet.'

'Oh god,' Sunny said. 'You two are going to be all loved up and I'm going to be the loser gooseberry.'

'Not if you go out with Sam . . .' Hannah said, bumping her with her arm.

'Yeah, that's not happening,' Sunny said. 'Nice to know he likes me though.'

The three of them started walking along the edge of the water, dodging the waves that seemed determined to soak the shoes they'd forgotten to take off in their hurry to talk.

Hannah said, 'Wouldn't your parents let you –'

'No, they wouldn't,' Sunny interrupted. 'So what's Dylan like then?' she asked Kitty.

'She's really cool,' Kitty said.

'I just realised – we saw her in Starbucks!' Hannah said.

'What?'

'We saw her in Starbucks! A couple of weeks ago. She said hello to you! I asked you who she was!'

Kitty blushed. 'Yeah. That's her.'

'Were you seeing her then?' Sunny asked.

'No!' Kitty said. 'I'd seen her there before – and I'd seen her round by my gran's – but I hadn't spoken to her or anything. I just . . . I thought she looked interesting. Different.'

'Does she go to Whiteacre?' Hannah asked.

Kitty nodded.

'I thought so,' Hannah said. 'You can just tell.'

'What does that mean?' Kitty asked.

'I don't know . . . I think . . . they just seem more confident. I mean, they stand out because they don't wear uniform, but also they just seem, I don't know . . . older.'

'She is a bit older,' Kitty said. 'She's just turned fifteen.'

'Ooh,' Sunny said. 'A cougar!'

'Oh my god,' Kitty said, laughing. 'As if.'

'I can't believe you thought we'd be upset,' Sunny said, suddenly serious.

Kitty shook her head. 'Me neither. I'm sorry. I've been freaking out a bit lately.'

'It's okay,' Hannah said. 'You've got a lot going on.'

'So you're not . . .' Kitty shook her head. She couldn't find the right word.

'Bothered?' Hannah said. 'God, no. Did you think we would be?'

'Why would you think that?' Sunny said.

'Because I've been hiding it from you,' Kitty said quietly. 'And we're best friends and I lied to you and the longer I didn't say anything, the harder it felt to say anything, especially when I wasn't even really sure myself.'

'God, Kitty,' Hannah said. 'You should know us better than that.'

Kitty's eyes filled with tears. She opened her mouth to speak, but didn't get a chance to because her two best friends threw themselves at her and almost knocked her off her feet with their hug. A rogue wave swept up the beach and soaked their feet. They all shrieked and ran to the steps.

'So when can we meet her? Dylan?' Hannah asked, once they were back on dry land.

'Soon,' Kitty said.

26

'I'm really nervous,' Kitty said, as she walked with Hannah and Sunny along the pier towards the Victorian sun lounge at the far end. Their families were coming too, but the three girls had agreed that they wanted to get there first, together.

Sunny squeezed Kitty's arm. 'Don't be nervous. It's going to be brilliant.'

'I'm as nervous about you two meeting Dylan as I am about the competition . . . If she comes.'

'Well I don't blame you for that,' Hannah said, laughing. 'But she'll come.'

'I hope so,' Kitty said. They'd talked on the phone. She'd told Dylan what had happened at school and then about her conversation with Hannah and Sunny, and everything seemed to be okay, but Kitty was worried anyway.

'We'll be nice, honest,' Sunny said. 'Well I will be. I can't wait to meet her.'

The butterflies in Kitty's stomach were making her feel sick, but it was such a nice evening – the light was almost golden and the river glittered in the sunlight – and she was with her best friends and about to – she hoped – meet her girlfriend.

She didn't even care if they didn't win the competition. Although that would be the icing on the cake.

At the far end of the sun lounge, under the glazed part, a low stage had been set up with rows of red, yellow and blue deckchairs lined up in front of it.

A woman from the council gave the three of them name tags – with their names and the name of the school – and showed them to the front row. Mrs Savage and Ms Guyomar were there already and both beamed at them.

'Excited, girls?' Mrs Savage said.

'Nervous,' Kitty said, her voice almost a squeak.

'You've done a wonderful job,' she said. 'It doesn't matter if you don't win.'

'Thanks for the vote of confidence,' Hannah whispered in Kitty's ear.

The screens at the back of the small stage were decorated with still photos from all the videos and Kitty could just make out herself, Sunny and Hannah in their fifties outfits. Just seeing the photo made her feel more confident. She really did think they'd made a good film. If there was a better one, fine. She was happy with what they'd done.

She glanced around, but couldn't see Dylan, so settled back in the chair to wait for the event to start.

'How long is this meant to take?' Sunny asked.

'Not sure,' Kitty said. 'Not long.'

'Oh my lot's here!' Sunny said. 'I hope they don't show me up. I thought about telling them the wrong time . . .'

Kitty turned to look and saw Sunny's mum, dad, sister and brother all lined up at the entrance, grinning and waving.

'I can't even pretend they're not with me,' Sunny said. 'We're the only Asians here.'

Kitty laughed. 'Why would you want to pretend they're not with you? They're awesome.'

'They're embarrassing,' Sunny said, turning back to look at the stage.

'Is your mum coming?' Kitty asked Hannah.

Hannah shook her head. 'Nope.'

'You did tell her about it?'

Hannah looked past Kitty towards the entrance. 'I left a note on the fridge.'

Kitty squeezed Hannah's arm. 'I'm sorry.'

'Look,' Hannah said, pointing.

Kitty looked. Her eyes filled with tears. Her mum, dad, Grace, Gran and . . . Tom.

'Oh my god!' Kitty tried to jump out of her seat, but it was next to impossible to jump out of a deckchair. She struggled to her feet and ran around the seats to throw herself at her brother.

'I couldn't miss this,' Tom said, squeezing her.

'I can't believe you're here!' Kitty said. 'Did you win the lottery?'

'Got some weekend work,' Tom said. 'Don't worry about it.'

'But you've got enough with uni work and –'

'I said don't worry about it!' Tom said, ruffling her hair because he knew it drove her mad. 'This is your day. Of course I wasn't going to miss it. If it takes me another year to graduate . . .'

She shoved him, thrilled he'd done whatever it was he'd done in order to be there for her.

She hugged her dad and her mum – who, she noticed, was hanging on quite tightly to her dad's arm. Grace was hopping up and down as if she was about to wet herself.

'Excited, Grace?' Kitty asked.

'No. Need the loo!'

Kitty laughed.

'I'll take her,' Kitty's gran said. They headed to the loos at the back of the lounge, while Kitty watched her dad and Tom help her mum into one of the deckchairs.

'I think I'll need a crane to get me back out of this,' her mum said, grimacing. She looked much better though. She'd been sitting out in the garden every morning with a cup of coffee and she looked healthier and happier than she had for months.

'I could go and find you a different chair?' Kitty suggested.

Her mum smiled at her. 'No. Thank you, but I'll be okay. Come and sit down a sec.'

Kitty flopped into the chair next to her mum's. Deckchairs really were stupid things.

'I just wanted to tell you – before it all starts – how proud of you I am,' her mum said.

'We both are,' her dad added. 'And not just about the film.'

Kitty had to bite the inside of her cheek to stop herself from crying – if they did win, she didn't want to have to go up on stage with fish eyes.

'I know things have been really hard,' her mum

said, 'but they're going to get better, I promise. And not just because I think you're going to win.'

Kitty laughed.

'But even if you don't,' her mum continued, 'we're so proud of you, Kitty. We want you to know that.'

'I do,' Kitty said, wiping under her eyes with her thumbs.

'Uh-oh,' her dad said. 'Better get back to your front row seat!'

Kitty looked over at the stage to see a couple of men in suits, the local Mayor and the woman she knew was one of the judges had stepped up on to the platform. One of the men was fiddling with the microphone.

Kitty leaned over and kissed her mum, then scurried back to her seat between Hannah and Sunny.

'Is Dylan here?' Hannah whispered.

Kitty shook her head. She fiddled with Dylan's scarf, which she'd tied around her wrist. Maybe Dylan wasn't going to come. There was nothing she could do about that now. She was about to look around one last time when the man on the stage spoke, the microphone screeching like nails on a blackboard. Everyone winced.

'Sorry,' he said. 'I'm Mike Furness from St Margaret's council. I'm honoured to be here this evening to announce the winners of the competition we've all been so excited about.'

He talked for a while about how strong the entries had been, about how they hadn't expected the standard to be so high, how they were thrilled that the competition had captured people's imaginations. He talked until people started to shuffle in their seats, the deckchairs creaking ominously.

Finally, they showed the videos. The first started with photos of St Margaret's tourist attractions with slow music over the top, then text came up on screen: *But that's not all!* The rest of the video had funky music and clips of the more alternative places in St Margaret's, like the skate park, nightclubs and even the pole-dancing class at the Albert Hotel.

The next one started really well – a collage of photos of St Margaret's with *Welcome to St Margaret's* over the top, but then it just cut between short clips of all the pretty places. The same pretty places that had appeared in the last video.

Their video was shown next. Kitty felt slightly embarrassed when it first started – not least because Sunny's family all whooped and cheered – but Kitty found she still loved it. She was still proud of it. And it was so much better than the other two.

The final video was like a music video. It had been filmed in the Lanes with loads of kids from Somerville School walking down the road and miming along with the song while pointing out the different shops and businesses. It was really good and the audience clapped along.

'Crap,' Hannah whispered in Kitty's ear.

'It's really good!' Kitty whispered back.

'That's what I mean,' Hannah said. 'Crap, it's really good.'

'I like ours better,' Sunny hissed.

Kitty shook her head. She didn't know. They were both so much better than the other two, but she honestly didn't know which of the two the judges would go for.

The film finished, the lights came back on and the woman judge stepped up to the microphone.

'All of the shortlisted videos were excellent, I'm sure you'll agree. But two really stood out for us: Quarry Mount and Somerville. It was incredibly hard to choose between them. Both videos were entertaining, accomplished and showed St Margaret's off beautifully. Exactly what we asked for, in fact. But one video was more original. And for that reason, our winning video is "Step into the Future" by Kitty, Hannah and Sunny of Quarry Mount High School.'

27

Kitty was still blushing from being up on the stage – even though it was only about half a metre off the ground – when she spotted Dylan. She was standing at the back, leaning against the glazed wall and grinning at Kitty. Kitty hadn't thought she could feel any more nervous than she already did, but the butterflies that had settled down burst back into life.

'Excuse me,' Kitty said to the person she was talking to – the mum of one of the other entrants who wanted to tell her all about St Margaret's when she was Kitty's age. 'I've just got to go and see . . .'

She half realised, as she crossed the lounge, that she'd probably just been really rude, but she didn't care. She just wanted to get to Dylan.

'Hey,' she said when she reached her.

'Hi,' Dylan said, smiling back. 'Congratulations.'

Kitty grinned. 'I can't believe we won!'

'I can,' Dylan said. 'Your video was brilliant.'

They smiled at each other.

'I'm so sorry, Dylan,' Kitty said.

Dylan shook her head. 'I know. You've said. It's okay.'

'Really?' Kitty said. She looked at Dylan's purple and red hair. At the earring in the top of her ear. At her eyeliner with the flicked up ends. She was wearing the dress she'd told Kitty about – pink satin with lace and leather. She looked beautiful.

'Really. I freaked out a bit too. Remember I said Tilda didn't like PDAs – I was worried that it was going to be like Tilda all over again and that didn't go so well, you know?' She smiled, wryly. 'But you're not her. You're you.'

Kitty smiled. 'I am.'

Dylan leaned forward and spoke close to Kitty's ear. 'Can I hug you?'

Kitty shook her head. 'No,' she said, stepping forward. 'I'll hug you.'

She wrapped her arms around Dylan and breathed in the mandarin scent of her hair and the mint that may or may not have been toothpaste.

'I'm so proud of you,' Dylan said in her ear.

Kitty stepped back and looked at Dylan. Her girlfriend. Maybe. Hopefully. She could see the reflection of the fairy lights flickering in her brown eyes. Dylan smiled at her like there was no one else in the room. Kitty felt like there *was* no one else in the room.

'You want to kiss me, don't you?' Dylan said.

Kitty nodded.

And then she kissed her.

Kitty, Sunny and Hannah's stories
continue in

SPOTLIGHT ON SUNNY

out Spring 2015.

But you can get a sneak peek at book 2
right now!

Head to
www.scribd.com/CatnipBooks
to download an exclusive extract.

Acknowledgements

As always, I have so many people to thank, but the first one has to be Jim Dean for the blog post that gave me the opportunity to write this book in the first place. Thanks, Jim!

Huge thanks to my fabulous agent, Hannah Sheppard; to Non Pratt for being excited about Kitty, Sunny and Hannah's stories; and to Liz Bankes for the most fantastic edit notes that not only made me laugh out loud but also, importantly, didn't make me cry (much). And thank you to Tim Rose for the gorgeous cover.

Thank you to Lily Webber for the email that inspired the film competition in the book (and for answering my many many questions). (You know I'll have even more for the next book, right?)

Thanks to Iffath Ahmed for squeeing and loving the idea of Sunny right from the start; to Stephanie Burgis for reading and raving and making me cry; and to Fatima Patel and Selina McEntee for answering questions and correcting errors (any remaining errors are mine, obvs).

Thank you Sarah Painter for always responding to my flaily emails with encouragement, support and excellent advice (and for skipping Helen Fielding).

Thanks to all the brilliant book bloggers including Raimy Greenland, Laura Heath, Sophie Waters, Kirsty Connor, Michelle Cardozo, and the powerhouse that is Lucy Powrie. And thanks, of course, to all my wonderful readers, whose emails make me go 'Pfft. Shurrup!' with giddiness.

I'm particularly lucky to have the most fabulous author friends. The YA Think writers make me spit tea daily, and I'd be lost without writer besties Susie Day, Keren David, Luisa Plaja, Sophia Bennett, Cat Clarke and Tamsyn Murray. A special thank you to Rainbow Rowell for Twitter chats, beautiful books, and Girl Scout Cookies when I needed them most.

Finally, sloppy, squashy thank yous to David, Harry and Joe, who are just the best of everything.

Find out more about Keris and her books here:
www.keris–stainton.com
@keris

To discover more funny and fabulous reads,
follow the cat . . .

www.catnippublishing.co.uk